HORRID HENRY

Francesca Simon spent her childhood on the beach in California, and then went to Yale and Oxford Universities to study medieval history and literature. She now lives in London with her family. She has written over fifty books and won the Children's Book of the Year in 2008 at the Galaxy British Book Awards for *Horrid Henry and the Abominable Snowman*.

Tony Ross is one of Britain's best-known illustrators, with many picture books to his name as well as line drawings for many fiction titles. He lives in Oxfordshire.

Also by Francesca Simon
Don't Cook Cinderella
Helping Hercules

For younger readers
Café at the Edge of the Moon
Mr P's Naughty Book
The Parent Swap Shop
Illustrated by Pete Williamson

Spider School
Illustrated by Tony Ross

Barnyard Hullabaloo
Billy the Kid Goes Wild
Chicks Just Want to Have Fun
Mish Mash Hash
Moo Baa Baa Quack
Runaway Duckling
Where are my Lambs?
The Haunted House of Buffin Street
Jogger's Big Adventure
Look at Me
Meet the Gang
Miaow Miaow Bow Wow
Rampage in Prince's Garden
Yum Yum
The Topsy Turvies
Illustrated by Emily Bolam

There is a complete list of **Horrid Henry** titles at the end of the book.

Visit Horrid Henry's website at **www.horridhenry.co.uk** for competitions, games, downloads and a monthly newsletter!

A GREEDY GULP OF HORRID HENRY

Francesca Simon
Illustrated by Tony Ross

Orion
Children's Books

ORION CHILDREN'S BOOKS

This collection first published in Great Britain in 2011 by Orion Children's Books
This edition published in 2016 by Hodder and Stoughton

9 10

A CIP catalogue record for this book
is available from the British Library.

ISBN 978 1 4440 0096 2

Printed and bound in Great Britain
by Clays Ltd, St Ives plc

The paper and board used in this book are
made from wood from responsible sources.

MIX
Paper from
responsible sources
FSC® C104740

Orion Children's Books
An imprint of
Hachette Children's Group
Part of Hodder and Stoughton
Carmelite House
50 Victoria Embankment
London EC4Y 0DZ

An Hachette UK Company
www.hachette.co.uk

www.hachettechildrens.co.uk
www.horridhenry.co.uk

CONTENTS

HORRID HENRY AND THE ABOMINABLE SNOWMAN

For my niece, Ava Rose

CONTENTS

1

HORRID HENRY AND THE [redacted]LE SNOWMAN

Mood[redacted]im.

Thwack[redacted]

A snowball w[redacted]past and smacked Sour Susan in the face.

'AAAAARRGGHHH!' shrieked Susan.

'Ha ha, got you,' said Margaret.

'You big meanie,' howled Susan, scooping up a fistful of snow and hurling it at Margaret.

Thwack!

Susan's snowball smacked Moody Margaret in the face.

'OWWWW!' screamed Margaret.

'You've blinded me.'

'Good!' screamed Susan.

'I hate you!' shouted Margaret, shoving Susan.

'I hate you more!' shouted Susan, pushing Margaret.

Splat! Margaret toppled

Splat! Susan topple

'I'm going home

snowman,' sobbed

'Fine. I'll win withou you,' said Margaret.

'Won't!'

'Will! I'm going to win, copycat,' shrieked Margaret.

'*I'm* going to win,' shrieked Susan. 'I kept my best ideas secret.'

'Win? Win what?' demanded Horrid Henry, stomping down his front steps in his snow boots and swaggering over. Henry could hear the word *win* from miles away.

'Haven't you heard about the competition?' said Sour Susan. 'The prize is—'

'Shut up! Don't tell him,' shouted Moody Margaret, packing snow onto her snowman's head.

Win? Competition? Prize? Horrid Henry's ears quivered. What secret were they trying to keep from him? Well, not for long. Horrid Henry was an expert at extracting information.

'Oh, the competition. I know all about *that*,' lied Horrid Henry. 'Hey, great snowman,' he added, strolling casually over to Margaret's snowman and pretending to admire her work.

Now, what should he do? Torture? Margaret's ponytail was always a tempting target. And snow down her jumper would make her talk.

What about blackmail? He could spread some great rumours about Margaret at school. Or . . .

'Tell me about the competition or the ice guy gets it,' said Horrid Henry suddenly, leaping over to the snowman and putting his hands round its neck.

'You wouldn't dare,' gasped Moody Margaret.

Henry's mittened hands got ready to push.

'Bye bye, head,' hissed Horrid Henry. 'Nice knowing you.'

Margaret's snowman wobbled.

'Stop!' screamed Margaret. 'I'll tell you. It doesn't matter 'cause you'll never ever win.'

'Keep talking,' said Horrid Henry warily, watching out in case Susan tried to ambush him from behind.

'Frosty Freeze are having a best snowman competition,' said Moody Margaret, glaring. 'The winner gets a year's free supply of ice cream. The judges will decide tomorrow morning.

Now get away from my snowman.'

Horrid Henry walked off in a daze, his jaw dropping. Margaret and Susan pelted him with snowballs but Henry didn't even notice. Free ice cream for a year direct from the Frosty Freeze Ice Cream factory. Oh wow! Horrid Henry couldn't believe it. Mum and Dad were so mean and horrible they hardly ever let him have ice cream. And when they did, they never *ever* let him put on his own hot fudge sauce and whipped cream and sprinkles. Or even scoop the ice cream himself. Oh no.

Well, when he won the Best Snowman Competition they couldn't stop him gorging on Chunky Chocolate Fab Fudge Caramel Delight, or Vanilla Whip Tutti-Fruitti Toffee Treat. Oh boy! Henry could taste that glorious ice cream now. He'd live on ice cream. He'd bathe in ice cream. He'd sleep in ice cream. Everyone from school would turn up at his house when the Frosty Freeze truck arrived bringing his weekly barrels. No matter how much they begged, Horrid Henry would send them all away. No way was he sharing a drop of his precious ice cream with *anyone*.

And all he had to do was to build the best snowman in the neighbourhood. Pah! Henry's was sure to be the winner. He would build the biggest snowman of all. And not just a snowman. A snowman with claws, and horns, and fangs. A vampire-demon-monster snowman. An

Abominable Snowman. Yes!

Henry watched Margaret and Susan rolling snow and packing their saggy snowman. Ha. Snow heap, more like.

'You'll never win with *that*,' jeered Horrid Henry. 'Your snowman is pathetic.'

'Better than yours,' snapped Margaret.

Horrid Henry rolled his eyes.

'Obviously, because I haven't started mine yet.'

'We've got a big head start on you, so ha ha ha,' said Susan. 'We're building a ballerina snowgirl.'

'Shut up, Susan,' screamed Margaret.

A ballerina snowgirl? What a stupid idea. If that was the best they could do Henry was sure to win.

'Mine will be the biggest, the best, the most gigantic snowman ever seen,' said Horrid Henry. 'And much better than your stupid snow dwarf.'

'Fat chance,' sneered Margaret.

'Yeah, Henry,' sneered Susan. 'Ours is the best.'

'No way,' said Horrid Henry, starting to roll a gigantic ball of snow for Abominable's big belly. There was no time to lose.

Roll.

Roll.

Roll.

Up the path, down the path, across the garden, down the side, back and forth, back and forth, Horrid Henry rolled the biggest ball of snow ever seen.

'Henry, can I build a snowman with you?' came a little voice.

'No,' said Henry, starting to carve out some clawed feet.

'Oh please,' said Peter. 'We could build a great big one together. Like a bunny snowman, or a—'

'No!' said Henry. 'It's *my* snowman. Build your own.'

'Muuuummmm!' wailed Peter. 'Henry won't let me build a snowman with him.'

'Don't be horrid, Henry,' said Mum. 'Why don't you build one together?'

'NO!!!' said Horrid Henry. He wanted to make his *own* snowman.

If he built a snowman with his stupid worm brother, he'd have to share the prize. Well, no way. He wanted all that ice cream for himself. And his Abominable Snowman was sure to be the best. Why share a prize when you didn't have to?

'Get away from my snowman, Peter,' hissed Henry.

Perfect Peter snivelled. Then he started to roll a tiny ball of snow.

'And get your own snow,' said Henry. 'All this is mine.'

'Muuuuuum!' wailed Peter. 'Henry's hogging all the snow.'

★

'We're done,' trilled Moody Margaret. 'Beat *this* if you can.'

Horrid Henry looked at Margaret and Susan's snowgirl, complete with a big pink tutu wound round the waist. It was as big as Margaret.

'That old heap of snow is nothing compared to *mine*,' bragged Horrid Henry.

Moody Margaret and Sour Susan looked at Henry's Abominable Snowman, complete with Viking horned helmet, fangs, and hairy scary claws. It was a few centimetres taller than Henry.

'Nah nah ne nah nah, mine's bigger,' boasted Henry.

'Nah nah ne nah nah, mine's better,' boasted Margaret.

'How do you like *my* snowman?' said Peter. 'Do you think *I* could win?'

Horrid Henry stared at Perfect Peter's tiny snowman. It didn't even have a head, just a long, thin, lumpy body with two stones stuck in the top for eyes.

Horrid Henry howled with laughter.

'That's the worst snowman I've ever seen,' said Henry. 'It doesn't even have a head. That's a snow carrot.'

'It is not,' wailed Peter. 'It's a big bunny.'

'Henry! Peter! Suppertime,' called Mum.

Henry stuck out his tongue at Margaret.

'And don't you dare touch my snowman.'

Margaret stuck out her tongue at Henry.

'And don't you dare touch *my* snowgirl.'

'I'll be watching you, Margaret.'

'I'll be watching *you*, Henry.'

They glared at each other.

Henry woke.

What was that noise? Was Margaret sabotaging his snowman? Was Susan stealing his snow?

Horrid Henry dashed to the window.

Phew. There was his Abominable Snowman, big as ever, dwarfing every other snowman in the street. Henry's was definitely the biggest, and the best. Umm boy, he could taste that Triple Fudge Gooey Chocolate Chip Peanut Butter Marshmallow Custard ice cream right now.

Horrid Henry climbed back into bed.

A tiny doubt nagged him.

Was his snowman *definitely* bigger than Margaret's?

'Course it was, thought Henry.

'Are you sure?' rumbled his tummy.

'Yeah,' said Henry.

'Because I really want that ice cream,' growled his tummy. 'Why don't you double-check?'

Horrid Henry got out of bed.

He was sure his was bigger and better than Margaret's. He was absolutely sure his was bigger and better.

But what if—

I can't sleep without checking, thought Henry.

Tip toe.

Tip toe.

Tip toe.

Horrid Henry slipped out of the front door.

The whole street was silent and white and frosty. Every house had a snowman in front. All of them much smaller than Henry's, he noted with satisfaction.

And there was his Abominable Snowman looming up, Viking horns scraping the sky. Horrid Henry gazed at him proudly. Next to him was Peter's pathetic pimple, with its stupid black stones. A snow lump, thought Henry.

Then he looked over at Margaret's snowgirl. Maybe it had fallen down, thought Henry hopefully. And if it hadn't maybe he could help it on its way . . .

He looked again. And again. That evil fiend!

Margaret had sneaked an extra ball of snow on top, complete with a huge flowery hat.

That little cheater, thought Horrid Henry indignantly. She'd sneaked out after bedtime and made hers bigger than his. How dare she? Well, he'd fix Margaret. He'd add more snow to his right away.

Horrid Henry looked around. Where could he find more snow? He'd already used up every drop on his front lawn to build his giant, and no new snow had fallen.

Henry shivered.

Brr, it was freezing. He needed more snow, and he needed it fast. His slippers were starting to feel very wet and cold.

Horrid Henry eyed Peter's pathetic lump of snow. Hmmn, thought Horrid Henry.

Hmmn, thought Horrid Henry again.

Well, it's not doing any good sitting

there, thought Henry. Someone could trip over it. Someone could hurt themselves. In fact, Peter's snowlump was a danger. He had to act fast before someone fell over it and broke a leg.

Quickly, he scooped up Peter's

snowman and stacked it carefully on top of his. Then standing on his tippy toes, he balanced the Abominable Snowman's Viking horns on top.

Da dum!

Much better. And *much* bigger than Margaret's.

Teeth chattering, Horrid Henry sneaked back into his house and crept into bed. Ice cream, here I come, thought Horrid Henry.

Ding dong.

Horrid Henry jumped out of bed. What a morning to oversleep.

Perfect Peter ran and opened the door.

'We're from the Frosty Freeze Ice Cream Factory,' said the man, beaming. 'And you've got the winning snowman out front.'

'I won!' screeched Horrid Henry. 'I won!' He tore down the stairs and out the door. Oh what a lovely lovely day. The sky was blue. The sun was shining — huh???

Horrid Henry looked around.

Horrid Henry's Abominable Snowman was gone.

'Margaret!' screamed Henry. 'I'll kill you!'

But Moody Margaret's snowgirl was gone, too.

The Abominable Snowman's helmet lay on its side on the ground. All that was left of Henry's snowman was . . . Peter's pimple, with its two black stone eyes. A big blue ribbon was pinned to the top.

'But that's *my* snowman,' said Perfect Peter.

'But . . . but . . .' said Horrid Henry.

'You mean, *I* won?' said Peter.

'That's wonderful, Peter,' said Mum.

'That's fantastic, Peter,' said Dad.

'All the others melted,' said the Frosty Freeze man. 'Yours was the only one left. It must have been a giant.'

'It was,' howled Horrid Henry.

2

HORRID HENRY'S RAINY DAY

Horrid Henry was bored. Horrid Henry was fed up. He'd been banned from the computer for rampaging through Our Town Museum. He'd been banned from watching TV just because he was caught watching a *teeny* tiny bit extra after he'd been told to switch it off straight after Mutant Max. Could he help it if an exciting new series about a rebel robot had started right after? How would he know if it were any good unless he watched some of it?

It was completely unfair and all Peter's fault for telling on him, and Mum and

Dad were the meanest, most horrible parents in the world.

And now he was stuck indoors, all day long, with absolutely nothing to do.

The rain splattered down. The house was grey. The world was grey. The universe was grey.

'I'm bored!' wailed Horrid Henry.

'Read a book,' said Mum.

'Do your homework,' said Dad.

'NO!' said Horrid Henry.

'Then tidy your room,' said Mum.

'Unload the dishwasher,' said Dad.

'Empty the bins,' said Mum.

'NO WAY!' shrieked Horrid Henry. What was he, a slave? Better keep out of his parents' way, or they'd come up with even more horrible things for him to do.

Horrid Henry stomped up to his boring bedroom and slammed the door. Uggh. He hated all his toys. He hated all his music. He hated all his games.

UGGGHHHHHH! What could he do?

Aha.

He could always check to see what Peter was up to.

Perfect Peter was sitting in his room arranging stamps in his stamp album.

'Peter is a baby, Peter is a baby,' jeered Horrid Henry, sticking his head round the door.

'Don't call me baby,' said Perfect Peter.

'OK, Duke of Poop,' said Henry.

'Don't call me Duke!' shrieked Peter.

'OK, Poopsicle,' said Henry.

'MUUUUM!' wailed Peter. 'Henry called me Poopsicle!'

'Don't be horrid, Henry!' shouted Mum. 'Stop calling your brother names.'

Horrid Henry smiled sweetly at Peter.

'OK, Peter, 'cause I'm so nice, I'll let you make a list of ten names that you don't want to be called,' said Henry. 'And it will only cost you £1.'

£1! Perfect Peter could not believe his ears. Peter would pay much more than that never to be called Poopsicle again.

'Is this a trick, Henry?' said Peter.

'No,' said Henry. 'How dare you? I make you a good offer, and you accuse me. Well, just for that—'

'Wait,' said Peter. 'I accept.' He handed Henry a pound coin. At last, all those horrid names would be banned. Henry would never call him Duke of Poop again.

Peter got out a piece of paper and a pencil.

Now, let's see, what to put on the list, thought Peter. Poopsicle, for a start. And I hate being called Baby, and Nappy Face, and Duke of Poop. Peter wrote and wrote and wrote.

'OK, Henry, here's the list,' said Peter.

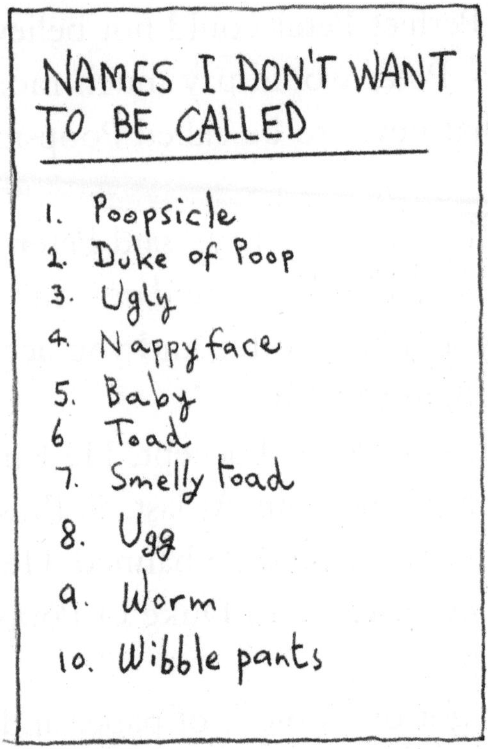
NAMES I DON'T WANT TO BE CALLED

1. Poopsicle
2. Duke of Poop
3. Ugly
4. Nappyface
5. Baby
6 Toad
7. Smelly toad
8. Ugg
9. Worm
10. Wibble pants

Horrid Henry scanned the list. 'Fine, pongy pants,' said Henry. 'Sorry, I meant poopy pants. Or was it smelly nappy?'

'MUUUMM!' wailed Peter. 'Henry's calling me names!'

'Henry!' screamed Mum. 'For the last time, can't you leave your brother alone?'

Horrid Henry considered. *Could* he leave that worm alone?

'Peter is a frog, Peter is a frog,' chanted Henry.

'MUUUUUUMMMMM!' screamed Peter.

'That's it, Henry!' shouted Mum. 'No pocket money for a week. Go to your room and stay there.'

'Fine!' shrieked Henry. 'You'll all be sorry when I'm dead.' He stomped down the hall and slammed his bedroom door as hard as he could. *Why* were his parents so mean and horrible? He was hardly bothering Peter at all. Peter *was* a frog. Henry was only telling the truth.

Boy would they be sorry when he'd died of boredom stuck up here.

If only we'd let him watch a little extra

TV, Mum would wail. Would that have been so terrible?

If only we hadn't made him do any chores, Dad would sob.

Why didn't I let Henry call me names, Peter would howl. After all, I do have smelly pants.

And now it's too late and we're sooooooo sorry, they would shriek.

But wait. *Would* they be sorry? Peter would grab his room. And all his best toys. His arch enemy Stuck-Up Steve could come over and snatch anything he wanted, even his skeleton bank and Goo-Shooter. Peter could invade the Purple Hand fort and Henry couldn't stop him. Moody Margaret could hop over the wall and nick his flag. And his biscuits. And his Dungeon Drink Kit. Even his . . . Supersoaker.

NOOOOOO!!!

Horrid Henry went pale. He had to stop those rapacious thieves. But how?

I could come back and haunt them, thought Horrid Henry. Yes! That would teach those grave-robbers not to mess with me.

'OOOOOOO, get out of my roooooooooom, you horrrrrrrible tooooooooooad,' he would moan at Peter.

'Touch my Gooooooo-shoooooter and you'll be morphed into ectoplasm,' he'd groan spookily from under Stuck-Up Steve's bed. Ha! That would show him.

Or he'd pop out from inside Moody Margaret's wardrobe.

'Giiiiive Henrrrrry's toyyyys back, you mis-er-a-ble sliiiiiimy snake,' he would rasp. That would teach her a thing or two.

Henry smiled. But fun as it would be to haunt people, he'd rather stop horrible

enemies snatching his stuff in the first place.

And then suddenly Horrid Henry had a brilliant, spectacular idea. Hadn't Mum told him just the other day that people wrote wills to say who they wanted to get all their stuff when they died? Henry had been thrilled.

'So when you die I get all your money!' Henry beamed. Wow. The house would be his! And the car! And he'd be boss of the TV, 'cause it would be his, too!!! And the only shame was—

'Couldn't you just give it all to me now?' asked Henry.

'Henry!' snapped Mum. 'Don't be horrid.'

There was no time to lose. He had to write a will immediately.

Horrid Henry sat down at his desk and grabbed some paper.

MY WILL
WARNING: DO NOT READ UNLESS I AM DEAD!!!!! I mean it!!!!

If you're reading this it's because I'm dead and you aren't. I wish you were dead and I wasn't, so I could have all *your* stuff. It's so not fair.

First of all, to anyone thinking of snatching my stuff just 'cause I'm dead . . . BEWARE! Anyone who doesn't do what I say will get haunted by a bloodless and boneless ghoul, namely me. So there.

Now the hard bit, thought Horrid Henry. Who should get his things? Was anyone deserving enough?

Peter, you are a worm. And a toad. And an ugly baby nappy face smelly ugg wibble pants poopsicle. I leave you . . . hmmmn. That toad really shouldn't get anything. But Peter was his brother after all.

I leave you my sweet wrappers. And a muddy twig.

That was more than Peter deserved. Still . . .

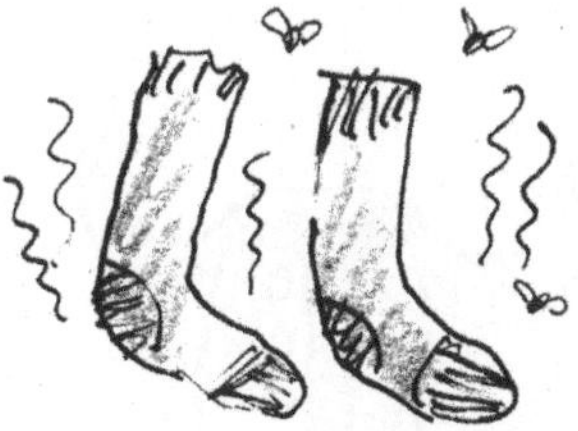

Steve, you are stuck-up and horrible and the world's worst cousin. You can have a pair of my socks. You can choose the blue ones with the holes or the falling down orange ones.

Margaret, you nit-face. I give you the Purple Hand flag to remember me by— NOT! You can have two radishes and the knight

with the chopped-off head. And keep your paws off my Grisly Grub Box!!! Or else . . .

Miss Battle-Axe, you are my worst teacher ever. I leave you a broken pencil.

Aunt Ruby, you can have the lime green cardigan back that you gave me for Christmas.

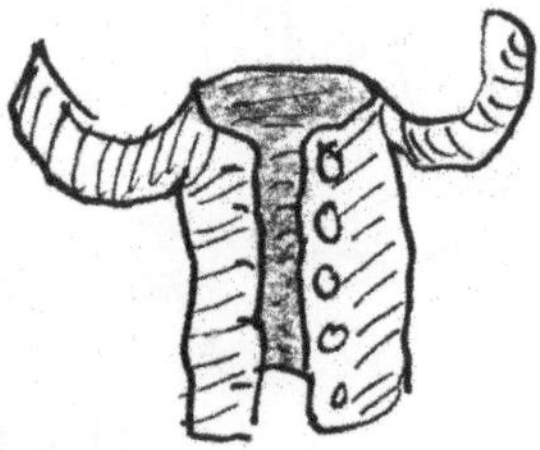

Hmmm. So far he wasn't doing so well giving away any of his good things.

Ralph, you can have my Goo-Shooter, but ONLY if you give *me* your football and your bike and your computer game Slime Ghouls.

That was more like it. After all, why should *he* be the only one writing a will?

It was certainly a lot more fun thinking about *getting* stuff from other people than giving away his own treasures.

In fact, wouldn't he be better off helping others by telling them what he wanted? Wouldn't it be awful if Rich Aunt Ruby left him some of Steve's old clothes in her will thinking that he would be delighted? Better write to her at once.

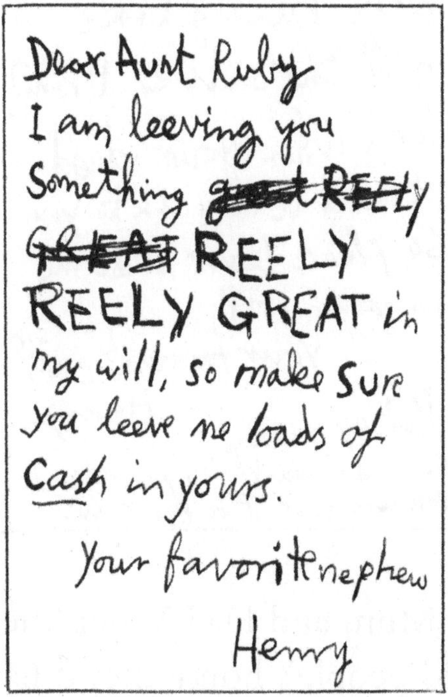

Dear Aunt Ruby
I am leeving you
Something ~~great~~ ~~REELY~~
~~GREAT~~ REELY
REELY GREAT in
my will, so make sure
you leeve me loads of
Cash in yours.
Your favoritenephew
Henry

Now, Steve. Henry was leaving him an old pair of holey socks. But Steve didn't have to *know* that, did he. For all Henry knew, Steve *loved* holey socks.

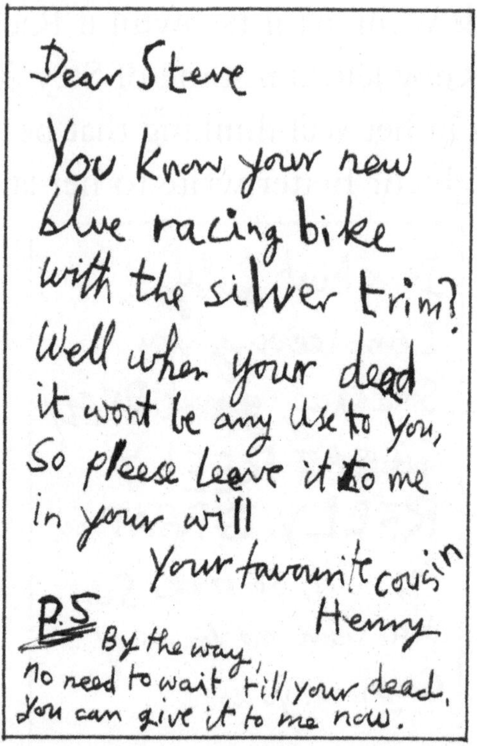

Dear Steve

You know your new blue racing bike with the silver trim? Well when your dead it wont be any Use to you, So pleese leave it to me in your will

Your favourite cousin
Henry

P.S By the way, no need to wait till your dead. You can give it to me now.

Right, Mum and Dad. When they were in the old people's home they'd hardly

need a thing. A rocking chair and blanket each would do fine for them.

So, how would Dad's music system look in his bedroom? And where could he put Mum's clock radio? Henry had always liked the chiming clock on their mantelpiece and the picture of the blackbird. Better go and check to see where he could put them.

Henry went into Mum and Dad's room, and grabbed an armload of stuff.

He staggered to his bedroom and dumped everything on the floor, then went back for a second helping.

Stumbling and staggering under his heavy burden, Horrid Henry swayed down the hall and crashed into Dad.

'What are you doing?' said Dad, staring. 'That's mine.'

'And those are mine,' said Mum.

'What is going on?' shrieked Mum and Dad.

'I was just checking how all this stuff will look in my room when you're in the old people's home,' said Horrid Henry.

'I'm not there yet,' said Mum.

'Put everything back,' said Dad.

Horrid Henry scowled. Here he was, just trying to think ahead, and he gets told off.

'Well, just for that I won't leave you any of my knights in my will,' said Henry.

Honestly, some people were so selfish.

3

MOODY MARGARET'S MAKEOVER

'Watch out, Gurinder! You're smearing your nail varnish,' screeched Moody Margaret. 'Violet! Don't touch your face – you're spoiling all my hard work. Susan! Sit still.'

'I am sitting still,' said Sour Susan. 'Stop pulling my hair.'

'I'm not pulling your hair,' hissed Margaret. 'I'm styling it.'

'Ouch!' squealed Susan. 'You're hurting me.'

'I am not, crybaby.'

'I'm not a crybaby,' howled Susan.

Moody Margaret sighed loudly.

'Not everyone can be naturally beautiful like me. Some people'– she glared at Susan – 'have to work at it.'

'You're not beautiful,' said Sour Susan, snorting.

'I am too,' said Margaret, preening herself.

'Are not,' said Susan. 'On the ugly scale of 1 to 10, with 1 being the ugliest, wartiest, toad, you're a 2.'

'Huh!' said Margaret. 'Well, *you're* so ugly you're minus 1. They don't have an ugly enough scale for *you*.'

'I want my money back!' shrieked Susan.

'No way!' shrieked Margaret. 'Now sit down and shut up.'

Across the wall in the next garden, deep inside the branches hiding the top secret entrance of the Purple Hand fort, a master spy pricked up his ears.

Money? Had he heard the word *money*?

What was going on next door?

Horrid Henry zipped out of his fort and dashed to the low wall separating his garden from Margaret's. Then he stared. And stared some more. He'd seen many weird things in his life. But nothing as weird as this.

Moody Margaret, Sour Susan, Lazy Linda, Vain Violet and Gorgeous Gurinder were sitting in Margaret's garden. Susan had rollers tangling her pink hair. Violet had blue mascara all over her face. Linda was covered in gold glitter. There was spilt nail varnish, face powder, and broken lipstick all over Margaret's patio.

Horrid Henry burst out laughing.

'Are you playing clowns?' said Henry.

'Huh, that's how much *you* know, Henry,' said Margaret. '*I'm* doing makeovers.'

'What's that?' said Henry.

'It's when you change how people look, dummy,' said Margaret.

'I knew that,' lied Henry. 'I just wanted to see if you did.'

Margaret waved a leaflet in his face.

MARGARET'S

MAGNIFICENT MAKEOVERS!

I can make *you* beautiful!

Yes, even YOU.

No one too old or too ugly.

Only £1 for a new you!!!!!

Hurry!

Special offer ends soon!!!!!!!!!!

Makeovers? *Makeovers?* What an incredibly stupid idea. Who'd pay to have a moody old grouch like Margaret smear gunk all over their face? Ha! No one.

Horrid Henry started laughing and pointing.

Vain Violet looked like a demon with red and blue and purple gloop all over her face. Gorgeous Gurinder looked as if a paint pot had been poured down her cheeks. Linda's hair looked as if she'd been struck by lightning.

But Violet wasn't screaming and yanking Margaret's hair out. Instead she handed Margaret—*money*.

'Thanks, Margaret, I look amazing,' said Vain Violet, admiring herself in the mirror. Henry waited for the mirror to crack.

It didn't.

'Thanks, Margaret,' said Gurinder. 'I look so fantastic I hardly recognise myself.' And she also handed Margaret a pound.

Two whole pounds? Were they mad?

'Are you getting ready for the Monster's Ball?' jeered Henry.

'Shut up, Henry,' said Vain Violet.

'Shut up, Henry,' said Gorgeous Gurinder.

'You're just jealous because I'm going to be rich and you're not,' said Margaret. 'Nah nah ne nah nah.'

'Why don't we give Henry a makeover?' said Violet.

'Good idea,' said Moody Margaret. 'He could sure use one.'

'Yeah,' said Sour Susan.

Horrid Henry took a step back.

Margaret advanced towards him wielding nail varnish and a hairbrush.

Violet followed clutching a lipstick, spray dye and other instruments of torture.

Yikes! Horrid Henry nipped back to the safety of his fort as fast as he could, trying to ignore the horrible, cackling laughter.

He sat on his Purple Hand throne and scoffed some extra tasty chocolate biscuits from the secret stash he'd nicked from Margaret yesterday. Makeovers! Ha! How dumb could you get? Trust a pea-brained grouch like Margaret to come up with such a stupid idea. Who in their right mind would want a makeover?

On the other hand . . .

Horrid Henry had actually seen Margaret being paid. And good money, too, just for smearing some coloured gunk onto people's faces and yanking their hair about.

Hmmmn.

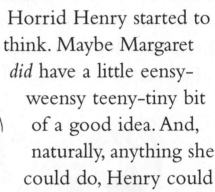

Horrid Henry started to think. Maybe Margaret *did* have a little eensy-weensy teeny-tiny bit of a good idea. And, naturally, anything she could do, Henry could do much, much better. Margaret obviously didn't know the first thing about makeovers, so why should *she* make all that money, thought Horrid Henry indignantly. He'd steal — no, *borrow* — her idea and do it better. Much much better. He'd make people look *really* fantastic.

Henry's Makeovers. Henry's Marvellous Makeovers. Henry's Miraculous Makeovers.

He'd be rich! With some false teeth and red marker he could turn Miss Battle-Axe into a vampire. Mrs Oddbod could be a perfect Dracula. And wouldn't Stuck-Up Steve be improved after a short visit from the Makeover Magician? Even Aunt Ruby wouldn't recognise him when Henry had finished. Tee hee.

First, he needed supplies. That was easy: Mum had tons of gunk for smearing all over her face. And if he ran out he could always use crayons and glue.

Horrid Henry dashed to the bathroom and helped himself to a few handfuls of Mum's makeup. What on earth did she need all this stuff for, thought Henry, piling it into a bag. About time someone cleared out this drawer. Then he wrote a few leaflets.

Horrid Henry, Makeover Magician, was ready for business.

All he needed were some customers. Preferably rich, ugly customers. Now, where could he find some of those?

Henry strolled into the sitting room. Dad was reading on the sofa. Mum was working at the computer.

Horrid Henry looked at his aged, wrinkly, boring old parents. Bleeeecccch!

Boy, could they be improved, thought

Henry. How could he tactfully persuade these potential customers that they needed his help – fast?

'Mum,' said Henry, 'you know Great-Aunt Greta?'

'Yes,' said Mum.

'Well, you're starting to look just like her.'

'What?' said Mum.

'Yup,' said Horrid Henry, 'old and ugly. Except—' he peered at her, 'you have more wrinkles.'

'*What?*' squeaked Mum.

'And Dad looks like a gargoyle,' said Henry.

'Huh?' said Dad.

'Only scarier,' said Henry. 'But don't worry, I can help.'

'Oh really?' said Mum.

'Oh really?' said Dad.

'Yeah,' said Henry, 'I'm doing makeovers.' He handed Mum and Dad a leaflet.

Are you ugly?

Are you very very ugly?

Do you look like the creature from the black lagoon? (Only worse?)

Then today is your lucky day!

HENRY'S

MARVELLOUS MAKEOVERS.

Only £2 for an exciting new you!!!!!!

'So, how many makeovers would you like?' said Horrid Henry. 'Ten? Twenty? Maybe more 'cause you're so old and need a lot of work to fix you.'

'Make over someone else,' said Mum, scowling.

'Make over someone else,' said Dad, scowling.

Boy, talk about ungrateful, thought Horrid Henry.

'Me first!'

'No me!'

Screams were coming from Margaret's garden. Kung-Fu Kate and Singing Soraya were about to become her latest victims. Well, not if Henry could help it.

'Step right up, get your makeovers here!' shouted Henry. 'Miracle Makeovers, from an expert. Only £2 for a brand new you.'

'Leave my customers alone, copycat!'

hissed Moody Margaret, holding out her hand to snatch Kate's pound.

Henry ignored her.

'You look boring, Kate,' said Henry. 'Why don't you let a *real* expert give you a makeover?'

'You?' said Kate.

'Two pounds and you'll look completely different,' said Horrid Henry. 'Guaranteed.'

'Margaret's only charging £1,' said Kate.

'My special offer today is 75p for the

first makeover,' said Henry quickly. 'And free beauty advice,' he added.

Soraya looked up. Kate stood up from Margaret's chair.

'Such as?' scowled Margaret. 'Go on, tell us.'

Eeeek. What on earth *was* a beauty tip? If your face is dirty, wash it? Use a nit comb? Horrid Henry had no idea.

'Well, in your case wear a bag over your head,' said Horrid Henry. 'Or a bucket.'

Susan snickered.

'Ha ha, very funny,' snapped Margaret. 'Come on, Kate. Don't let him trick you. *I'm* the makeover expert.'

'I'm going to try Henry,' said Kate.

'Me too,' said Soraya.

Yippee! His first customers. Henry

stuck out his tongue at Margaret.

Kung-Fu Kate and Singing Soraya climbed over the wall and sat down on the bench at the picnic table. Henry opened his makeover bag and got to work.

'No peeking,' said Henry. 'I want you to be surprised.'

Henry smeared and coated, primped and coloured, slopped and glopped. This was easy!

'I'm so beautiful — hoo hoo hoo,' hummed Soraya.

'Aren't you going to do my hair?' said Kung-Fu Kate.

'Naturally,' said Horrid Henry.

He emptied a pot of glue on her head and scrunched it around.

'What have you put in?' said Kate.

'Secret hair potion,' said Henry.

'What about *me*?' said Soraya.

'No problem,' said Henry, shovelling in some red paint.

A bit of black here, a few blobs of red there, a smear of purple and . . . way hey!

Henry stood back to admire his handiwork. Wow! Kung-Fu Kate looked *completely* different. So did Singing Soraya. Next time he'd charge £10. The moment people saw them everyone would want one of Henry's marvellous makeovers.

'You look amazing,' said Horrid Henry. He had no idea he was such a brilliant makeover artist. Customers would be queueing for his services. He'd need a bigger piggybank.

'There, just like the Mummy,

Frankenstein, *and* a vampire,' said Henry, handing Kate a mirror.

'AAAARRRRGGGGHHH!'

screamed Kung-Fu Kate.

Soraya snatched the mirror.

'AAAARRRRGGGGHHH!'

screamed Singing Soraya.

Horrid Henry stared at them. Honestly, there was no pleasing some people.

'NOOOOOOOOO'

squealed Kung-Fu Kate.

'But I thought you wanted to look amazing,' said Henry.

'Amazingly good! Not scary!' wailed Kate.

'Has anyone seen my new lipsticks?' said Mum. 'I could have sworn I put them in the—'

She caught sight of Soraya and Kate.

'AAAAAAARRRRRGGGGHHHH!'

screeched Mum. 'Henry! How could you be so horrid? Go to your room.'

'But . . . but . . . ' gasped Horrid Henry. It was so unfair. Was it his fault his stupid customers didn't know when they looked great?

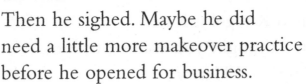

Henry stomped up the stairs.

Then he sighed. Maybe he did need a little more makeover practice before he opened for business.

Now, where could he find someone to practise on?

'I got an A on my spelling test,' said Perfect Peter.

'I got a gold star for having the tidiest drawer,' said Tidy Ted.

'And I got in the Good as Gold book again,' said Goody-Goody Gordon.

Henry burst into Peter's bedroom.

'I'm doing makeovers,' said Horrid Henry. 'Who wants to go first?'

'Uhhmmm,' said Peter.

'Uhhmmm,' said Ted.

'We're going to Sam's birthday party today,' said Gordon.

'Even better,' said Henry beaming. 'I can make you look great for the party. Who's first?'

TJ FIZZ
Ghost Ques
TJ FIZZ
TJ FIZZ
TJ FIZZ
TJ FIZZ
Ghouls Jewels
TJ FIZZ

4

HORRID HENRY'S AUTHOR VISIT

Horrid Henry woke up. He felt strange. He felt . . . happy. He felt . . . excited. But why?

Was it the weekend? No. Was it a day off school? No. Had Miss Battle-Axe been kidnapped by aliens and transported to another galaxy to slave in the salt mines? No (unfortunately).

So why was he feeling so excited on a school day?

And then Horrid Henry remembered.

Oh wow!! It was Book Week at Henry's school, and his favourite author in the whole world, TJ Fizz, the writer of the stupendous *Ghost Quest* and *Mad Machines* and *Skeleton Skunks* was coming to talk to his class. Henry had read every single one of TJ's brilliant books, even after lights out. Rude Ralph thought they were almost as good as Mutant Max comics. Horrid Henry thought they were even better.

Perfect Peter bounced into his room.

'Isn't it exciting, Henry?' said Perfect Peter. 'Our class is going to meet a real live author! Milksop Miles is coming today. He's the man who wrote *The Happy Nappy*. Do you think he'd sign my copy?'

Horrid Henry snorted.

The Happy Nappy! Only the dumbest book ever. All those giant nappies with names like Rappy Nappy and Zappy Nappy and Tappy Nappy dancing and prancing about. And then the truly

horrible Gappy Nappy, who was always wailing, 'I'm leaking!'

Horrid Henry shuddered. He was amazed that Milksop Miles dared to show his face after writing such a boring book.

'Only a wormy toad like you could like such a stupid story,' said Henry.

'It's not stupid,' said Peter.

'Is too.'

'Is not. And he's bringing his guitar. Miss Lovely said so.'

'Big deal,' said Horrid Henry. '*We've* got TJ Fizz.'

Perfect Peter shuddered.

'Her books are too scary,' said Peter.

'That's 'cause you're a baby.'

'Mum!' shrieked Peter. 'Henry called me baby.'

'Telltale,' hissed Henry.

'Don't be horrid, Henry,' shouted Mum.

Horrid Henry sat in class with a huge carrier bag filled with all his TJ Fizz books. Everyone in the class had drawn book covers for *Ghost Quest* and *Ghouls' Jewels,* and written their own *Skeleton Skunk* story. Henry's of course was the best: *Skeleton Skunk meets Terminator*

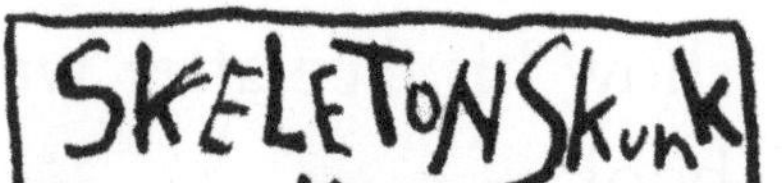

Gladiator: May the smelliest fighter win! He would give it to TJ Fizz if she paid him a million pounds.

Ten minutes to go. How could he live until it was time for her to arrive?

Miss Battle-Axe cleared her throat.

'Class, we have a very important guest coming. I know you're all very excited, but I will not tolerate anything but perfect behaviour today. Anyone who misbehaves will be sent out. Is that clear?' She glared at Henry.

Henry scowled back. Of course he would be perfect. TJ Fizz was coming!

'Has everyone thought of a good question to ask her? I'll write the best ones on the board,' continued Miss Battle-Axe.

'How much money do you make?' shouted Rude Ralph.

'How many TVs do you have?' shouted Horrid Henry.

'Do you like fudge?' shouted Greedy Graham.

'I said *good* questions,' snapped Miss Battle-Axe. 'Bert, what's your question for TJ Fizz?'

'I dunno,' said Beefy Bert.

Rumble.
Rumble.
Rumble.

Ooops. Henry's tummy was telling him it was snacktime.

It must be all the excitement. It was strictly forbidden to eat in class, but Henry was a master sneaker. He certainly wouldn't want his tummy to gurgle while TJ Fizz was talking.

Miss Battle-Axe was writing down Clever Clare's eight questions on the board.

Slowly, carefully, silently, Horrid Henry opened his lunchbox under the table. Slowly, carefully, silently, he eased open the bag of crisps.

Horrid Henry looked to the left.

Rude Ralph was waving his hand in the air.

Horrid Henry looked to the right.

Greedy Graham was drooling and opening a bag of sweets.

The coast was clear. Henry popped some Super Spicy Hedgehog crisps into his mouth.

MUNCH! CRUNCH!

'C'mon Henry, give me some crisps,' whispered Rude Ralph.

'No,' hissed Horrid Henry. 'Eat your own.'

'I'm starving,' moaned Greedy Graham. 'Gimme a crisp.'

'No!' hissed Horrid Henry.

MUNCH CRUNCH! YANK

Huh?

Miss Battle-Axe towered over him holding aloft his bag of crisps. Her red eyes were like two icy daggers.

'What did I tell you, Henry?' said Miss Battle-Axe. 'No bad behaviour would be tolerated. Go to Miss Lovely's class.'

'But . . . but . . . TJ Fizz is coming!' spluttered Horrid Henry. 'I was just—'

Miss Battle-Axe pointed to the door. 'Out!'

'NOOOOOOOOOO!' howled Henry.

Horrid Henry sat in a tiny chair at the back of Miss Lovely's room. Never had he suffered such torment. He tried to block his ears as Milksop Miles read his horrible book to Peter's class.

'Hello, Happy, Clappy and Yappy! Can *you* find the leak?'

'No,' said Happy.

'No,' said Clappy.

'No,' said Yappy.

'I can,' said Gappy Nappy.

AAAARRRRGGGGHHH! Horrid Henry gritted his teeth. He would go mad having to listen to this a moment longer.

He had to get out of here.

'All together now, let's sing the Happy Nappy song,' trilled Milksop Miles, whipping out his guitar.

'Yay!' cheered the infants.

No, groaned Horrid Henry.

Oh I'm a happy nappy,
a happy zappy nappy
I wrap up your bottom, snug and tight,
And keep you dry all through the night
Oh –

This was torture. No, this was worse than torture. How could he sit here listening to the horrible Happy Nappy song knowing that just above him TJ Fizz was reading from one of her incredible books, passing round the famous skunk skeleton, and showing off her *Ghost Quest* drawings. He had to get back to his own class. He had to.

But how?

What if he joined in the singing? He could bellow:

Oh I'm a soggy nappy
A smelly, stinky nappy–

Yes! That would certainly get him sent out the door straight to — the head. Not back to his class and TJ Fizz.

Horrid Henry closed his mouth. Rats.

Maybe there'd be an earthquake? A power failure? Where was a fire-drill when you needed one?

He could always pretend he needed the toilet. But then when he didn't come back they'd come looking for him.

Or maybe he could just sneak away? Why not? Henry got to his feet and began to slide towards the door, trying to be invisible.

Sneak **Sneak** **Sn –**

'Whooa, come back here, little boy,' shouted Milksop Miles, twanging his guitar. Henry froze. 'Our party is just starting. Now who knows the Happy Nappy dance?'

'I do,' said Perfect Peter.

'I do,' said Goody-Goody Gordon.

'We all do,' said Tidy Ted.

'Everyone on their feet,' said Milksop Miles. 'Ah-one ah-two, let's all do the Nappy Dance!'

'Nap nap nap nap nap nap nappy,' warbled Miles.

'Nap nap nap nap nap nap nappy,' warbled Peter's class, dancing away.

Desperate times call for desperate measures. Horrid Henry started dancing. Slowly, he tapped his way closer and closer and closer to the door and — freedom!

Horrid Henry reached for the door knob. Miss Lovely was busy dancing in the corner. Just a few more steps . . .

'Who's going to be my little helper while we act out the story?' beamed Miles. 'Who would like to play the Happy Nappy?'

'Me! Me!' squealed Miss Lovely's class.

Horrid Henry sank against the wall.

'Come on, don't be shy,' said Miles, pointing straight at Henry. 'Come on up and put on the magic happy nappy!' And he marched over and dangled an enormous blue nappy in front of Henry. It was over one metre wide and one metre high, with a hideous smiling face and big goggly eyes.

Horrid Henry took a step back. He felt faint. The giant nappy was looming above him. In a moment it would be over his head and he'd be trapped inside. His name would be mud — forever. Henry the nappy. Henry the giant nappy. Henry the giant happy nappy . . .

'**AAAARRRRGGGGHHH!**' screamed Horrid Henry. 'Get away from me!'

Milksop Miles stopped waving the gigantic nappy.

'Oh dear,' he said.

'Oh dear,' said Miss Lovely.

'Don't be scared,' said Miles.

Scared? Horrid Henry . . . scared? Of a giant nappy? Henry opened his mouth to scream.

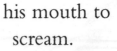

And then he stopped.

What if . . . ?

'Help! Help! I'm being attacked by a nappy!' screeched Henry. 'HELLLLLLLP!'

Milksop Miles looked at Miss Lovely. Miss Lovely looked at Milksop Miles.

'HELLLLLLLP! HELLLLLLLP!'

'Henry? Are you OK?' piped Perfect Peter.

'NOOOOOOOO!' wailed Horrid Henry, cowering. 'I'm . . . I'm . . . nappy-phobic.'

'Never mind,' said Milksop Miles. 'You're not the first boy who's been scared of a giant nappy.'

'I'm sure I'll be fine if I go back to my

own class,' gasped Horrid Henry.

Miss Lovely hesitated. Horrid Henry opened his mouth to howl —

'Run along then,' said Miss Lovely quickly.

Horrid Henry did not wait to be asked twice.

He raced out of Miss Lovely's class, then dashed upstairs to his own.

Skeleton Skunk here I come, thought Henry, bursting through the door.

There was the great and glorious TJ Fizz, just about to start reading a brand new chapter from her latest book, *Skeleton Stinkbomb*. Hallelujah, he was in time.

'Henry, what are you doing here?' hissed Miss Battle-Axe.

'Miss Lovely sent me back,' beamed Horrid Henry. 'And you did say we should be on our best behaviour today, so I did what I was told.'

Henry sat down as TJ began to read. The story was amazing.

Ahhh, sighed Horrid Henry happily, wasn't life grand?

HORRID HENRY
Robs The Bank

For my brilliant friend Dina Rabinovitch,
who did so much for children's literature,
and for her son, Elon Julius

CONTENTS

1

HORRID HENRY'S NEWSPAPER

'It's not fair!' howled Horrid Henry. 'I want a Hip-Hop Robot dog!'

Horrid Henry needed money. Lots and lots and lots of money. His parents didn't need money, and yet they had loads more than he did. It was so unfair. Why was he so brilliant at *spending* money, and so bad at *getting* money?

And now Mum and Dad refused to buy him something he desperately needed.

'You have plenty of toys,' said Mum.

'Which you never play with,' said Dad.

'That's 'cause they're all so boring!' screeched Henry. 'I want a robot dog!'

'Too expensive,' said Mum.

'Too noisy,' said Dad.

'But *everyone* has a Hip-Hop Robot Dog,' whined Henry. 'Everyone but *me*.'

Horrid Henry stomped out of the room. How could he get some money?

Wait. Maybe he could *persuade* Peter to give him some. Peter always had tons of cash because he never bought anything.

Yes! He could hold Peter's Bunnykins for ransom. He could tell Peter his room

was haunted and get Peter to pay him for ghostbusting. He could make Peter donate to Henry's favourite charity, Child in Need . . . Hip-Hop Robot Dog, here I come, thought Horrid Henry, bursting into Peter's bedroom.

Perfect Peter and Tidy Ted were whispering together on the floor. Papers were scattered all around them.

'You can't come in my room,' said Peter.

'Yes I can,' said Henry, ' 'cause I'm already in. Pooh, your room stinks.'

'That's 'cause you're in it,' said Peter.

Henry decided to ignore this insult.

'Whatcha doing?'

'Nothing,' said Peter.

'We're writing our own newspaper like Mrs Oddbod suggested in assembly,' said Ted. 'We've even got a *Tidy with Ted* column,' he added proudly.

'A snooze paper, you mean,' said Henry.

'It is not,' said Peter.

Henry snorted. 'What's it called?'

'The Best Boys' Busy Bee,' said Peter.

'What a stupid name,' said Henry.

'It's not a stupid name,' said Peter. 'Miss Lovely said it was perfect.'

'Peter, I have a great idea for your paper,' said Henry.

'What?' said Peter cautiously.

'You can use your newspaper for

Fluffy's cat litter tray.'

'MUUUM!' wailed Peter. 'Henry's being mean to me.'

'Don't be horrid, Henry!' shouted Mum.

'Peter is a poopsicle, Peter is a poopsicle,' chanted Henry.

But then Peter did something strange. Instead of screaming for Mum, Peter started writing.

'Now everyone who buys my newspaper will know how horrid you are,' said Peter, putting down his pencil.

Buy? *Buy?*

'We're selling it in school tomorrow,' said Ted. 'Miss Lovely said we could.'

Sell? *Sell?*

'Lemme see that,' said Henry, yanking the paper out of Peter's hands.

The *Busy Bee's* headline read:

PETER IN THE GOOD AS GOLD BOOK FOR THE FOURTH TIME THIS MONTH

Horrid Henry snorted. What a worm. Then his eye caught the second headline:

COMPUTER BAN FOR HORRID BOY

Henry was banned from playing games on the computer today because he was mean to his brother Peter and called him wibble pants and poopsicle. *The Busy Bee* hopes Henry has learned his lesson and will stop being such a big meanie.

'You're going to . . . *sell* this?' spluttered Henry. His name would be mud. Worse than mud. Everyone would know what a stupid toad brother he had. Worse, some people might even *believe* Peter's lies.

And then suddenly Horrid Henry had a brilliant, spectacular idea. He'd write his *own* newspaper. Everyone would want to buy it. He'd be rich!

He could call his newspaper *The Hourly Howler* and charge 25p a copy. If he could write seven editions a day, and sell each copy to 500 people, he'd make . . . he'd make . . . well, multiplication was never his best subject, but he could make *tons* of money!!!!!!

On the other hand, writing seven newspapers a day, every day, seemed an awful lot of work. An awful, awful lot of work. Perhaps *The Daily Digger* was the way to go. He'd charge a lot more per copy, and do a lot less work. Yes!

Hmmn. Perhaps *The Weekly Warble* would be better. No, *The Monthly Moaner.*

Maybe just *The Purple Hand Basher.*

The Basher! What a great name for a great paper!

Now, what should his newspaper have? News of course. All about Henry's triumphs. And gossip and quizzes and sport.

First, I need a great headline, thought Horrid Henry.

What about: PETER IS A WORM. Tempting, thought Henry, but old news: everyone already knows that Peter is a worm. What could he tell his readers that they *didn't* know?

After all, news didn't have to be true, did it? Just *new*. And boy did he have some brand-new news!

PETER SENT TO PRISON

The world's toadiest brother has been found guilty of being a worm and taken straight to prison. He was sentenced to live on bread and water for three years. *The Basher* says: 'It should have been ten years.'

SECRET CLUB COLLAPSES!!!

The Secret Club has collapsed. 'Margaret is such a moody old bossy-boots no one wants to be in her club any more,' said Susan.

'Goodbye, grump-face,' said Gurinder.

Right, that was the news section taken care of. Now, for some good gossip.

But what gossip? What scandal? Sadly, Horrid Henry didn't know any horrid rumours. But a gossip columnist needed to write something . . .

MRS ODDBOD BIKINI SHOCK

Mrs Oddbod was seen strolling down the High Street wearing a new yellow polka dot bikini. Is this any way for a head teacher to behave?

TEACHER IN TOILET TERROR

Terrible screams rang out from the boys' toilets yesterday. 'Help! Help! There's a monster in the loo!' screamed the crazed teacher Miss Boudicca Battle-Axe. 'It's got hairy scary claws and three heads!!'

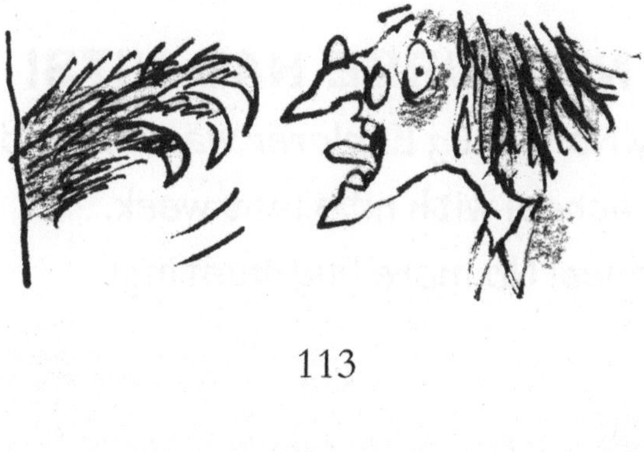

GUESS WHO?

Which soggy swimming teacher was seen dancing the cha-cha-cha with which old battle-axe?

MISS LOVELY IN NOSE PICK HORROR

Oh dear, Miss Lydia Lovely picks her nose.

'I saw her do it in class,' says Prisoner Peter.

'But she said it was her nose and she would pick it if she wanted to.'

NIT NURSE HAS NITS!

Nitty Nora, Bug Explorer was sent home from school with nits last week. Whoopee! No more bug-busting!

That's enough great gossip for one issue, thought Horrid Henry. Now, what else, what else? A bit about sports and he was done. In tomorrow's edition, he'd add a comic strip: The adventures of Peter the Nappy. And a quiz:

Who has the smelliest pants in school?
A. Peter
B. Margaret
C. Susan
D. All of the above!

Yippee! thought Horrid Henry. I'm going to be rich, rich, rich, rich, rich.

The next morning Henry made sure he got to school bright and early. Hip-hop Robot, here I come, thought Horrid Henry, lugging a huge pile of *Bashers* into the playground. Then he stopped.

A terrible sight met his eyes.

Moody Margaret and Sour Susan were standing in the school playground waving big sheets of paper.

'Step right up, read all about it, Margaret made Captain of the school football team,' bellowed Moody Margaret. 'Get your *Daily Dagger* right here. Only 25p!'

What a copycat, thought Horrid Henry. He was outraged.

'Who'd want to read *that*?' sneered Horrid Henry.

'Everyone,' said Susan.

Horrid Henry snatched a copy.

'That'll be 25p, Henry,' said Margaret.

Henry ignored her. The headline read:

MARGARET TRIUMPHS

Margaret, the best footballer in school history, beat out her puny opposition to

become captain of the school football team! Well done Margaret! Everyone cheered for hours when Mrs Oddbod announced the glorious news.

Margaret gave an exclusive interview to the *Daily Dagger*:

'It's hard being as amazing as I am,' said Margaret. 'So many people are jealous, especially pongy pants pimples like Henry.'

'What a load of rubbish,' said Horrid Henry, scrunching up Margaret's newspaper.

'Our customers don't think so,' said Margaret. 'I'm making *loads* of loot. Before you know it *I'll* have the first Hip-Hop Robot Dog. And you-ooooo won't,' she chanted.

'We'll see about that,' said Horrid Henry. 'Teacher in toilet terror! Read all about it!' he hollered. 'All the news and gossip. Only 25p.'

'News! News!' screeched Margaret. 'Step right up, step right up! Only 24p.'

'Buy the *Busy Bee!*' piped Peter. 'Only 5p.'

Rude Ralph bought a *Basher.* So did Dizzy Dave and Jolly Josh.

Lazy Linda approached Margaret.

'Oy, Linda, don't buy that rubbish,' shouted Henry. '*I've* got the best news and gossip.' Henry whispered in Linda's ear. Her jaw dropped and she handed Henry 25p.

'Don't listen to him!' squealed Margaret.

'Buy the *Busy Bee,*' trilled Perfect Peter. 'Free vegetable chart.'

'Margaret, did you see what Henry wrote about you?' gasped Gorgeous Gurinder.

'What?' said Margaret, grabbing a *Basher.*

SPORTS

SHOCK FOOTBALL NEWS

There was shock all round when Henry wasn't made captain of the school football team.

'It's an outrage,' said Dave.

'Disgusting,' said Soraya.

The Basher was lucky enough to get an exclusive interview with Henry.

'Not making me captain just goes to show what an idiot that old carrot-nose Miss Battle-Axe is,' says Henry.

The Basher says: **Make Henry captain!**

'What!' screamed Margaret. 'Dave and Soraya never said *that*.'

'They thought it,' said Henry. He glared at Moody Margaret.

Moody Margaret glared at Horrid Henry.

Henry's hand reached out to pull Margaret's hair.

Margaret's foot reached out to kick Henry's leg.

Suddenly Mrs Oddbod walked into the playground. There was a stern-looking man with her, wearing a suit and carrying a notebook. Miss Battle-Axe and Miss Lovely followed.

Aha, new customers, thought Horrid Henry, as they headed towards him.

'Get your school paper here!' hollered Henry. 'Only 50p.'

'News! News!' screeched Margaret.

'Step right up, step right up! 49p.'

'Buy the *Busy Bee*!' trilled Peter. 'Only 5p.'

'Well, well,' said the strange man. 'What have we here, Mrs Oddbod?'

Mrs Oddbod beamed. 'Just three of our best students showing how enterprising they are,' she said.

Horrid Henry thought his ears had fallen off. *Best* student? And why was Mrs Oddbod smiling at him? Mrs Oddbod *never* smiled at him.

'Peter, why don't you tell the inspector what you're doing,' said Miss Lovely.

'I've written my own newspaper to raise money for the school,' said Perfect Peter.

'Very impressive, Mrs Oddbod,' said the school inspector, smiling. 'Very impressive. And what about you, young man?' he added, turning to Henry.

'I'm selling my newspaper for a Child in Need,' said Horrid Henry. In need of a Hip-Hop Robot, he thought. 'How many do you want to buy?'

The school inspector handed over 50p and took a paper.

'I love school newspapers,' he said, starting to read. 'You find out so much about what's really happening at a school.'

The school inspector gasped. Then he turned to Mrs Oddbod.

'What do you know about a yellow polka dot bikini?' said the Inspector.

'Yellow . . . polka . . . dot . . . bikini?' said Mrs Oddbod.

'Cha-cha-cha?' choked Miss Battle-Axe.

'Nose-picking?' gasped Miss Lovely.

'But what's the point of writing news that everyone knows?' protested Horrid

Henry afterwards in Mrs Oddbod's office. 'News should be *new*.'

Just wait till tomorrow's edition . . .

2

MOODY MARGARET'S SCHOOL

'Pay attention, Susan,' shrieked Moody Margaret, 'or you'll go straight to the head.'

'I *am* paying attention,' said Sour Susan.

'This is boring,' said Horrid Henry. 'I want to play pirates.'

'Silence,' said Moody Margaret, whacking her ruler on the table.

'I want to be the teacher,' said Susan.

'No,' said Margaret.

'*I'll* be the teacher,' said Horrid Henry. He'd send the class straight out for play-time, and tell them to run for their lives.

'Are you out of your mind?' snapped Margaret.

'Can I be the teacher?' asked Perfect Peter.

'NO!' shouted Margaret, Susan, and Henry.

'Why can't I be the head?' said Susan sourly.

'Because,' said Margaret.

''cause why?' said Susan.

''cause *I'm* the head.'

'But you're the head *and* the teacher,' said Susan. 'It's not fair.'

'It is too fair, 'cause you'd make a terrible head,' said Margaret.

'Wouldn't!'

'Would!'

'I think we should take turns being head,' said Susan.

'That,' said Margaret, 'is the dumbest idea I've ever heard. Do you see Mrs

Oddbod taking *turns* being head? I don't think so.'

Margaret's class grumbled mutinously on the carpet inside the Secret Club tent.

'Class, I will now take the register,' intoned Margaret. 'Susan?'

'Here.'

'Peter?'

'Here.'

'Henry?'

'In the toilet.'

Margaret scowled.

'We'll try that again. Henry?'

'Flushed away.'

'Last chance,' said Margaret severely. 'Henry?'

'Dead.'

Margaret made a big cross in her register.

'I will deal with you later.'

'No one made *you* the big boss,' muttered Horrid Henry.

'It's *my* house and we'll play what *I* want,' said Moody Margaret. 'And I want to play school.'

Horrid Henry scowled. Whenever Margaret came to *his* house she was the guest and he had to play what *she* wanted. But whenever Henry went to her house Margaret was the boss 'cause it was *her* house. Ugggh. Why oh why did he have to live next door to Moody Margaret?

Mum had important work to do, and needed total peace and quiet, so Henry and Peter had been dumped at Margaret's. Henry had

begged to go to Ralph's, but Ralph was visiting his grandparents. Now he was trapped all day with a horrible, moody old grouch. Wasn't it bad enough being with Miss Battle-Axe all week without having to spend his whole precious Saturday stuck at Margaret's? And, even worse, playing school?

'Come on, let's play pirates,' said Henry. 'I'm Captain Hook. Peter, walk the plank!'

'No,' said Margaret. 'I don't want to.'

'But I'm the guest,' protested Henry.

'So?' said Margaret. 'This is *my* house

and we play by *my* rules.'

'Yeah, Henry,' said Sour Susan.

'And I love playing school,' said Perfect Peter. 'It's such fun doing sums.'

Grrr. If only Henry could just go home. 'I want a good report,' Mum had said, 'or you won't be going to Dave's bowling party tonight. It's very kind of Margaret and her mum to have you boys over to play.'

'But I don't want to go to Margaret's!' howled Henry. 'I want to stay home and watch TV!'

'N-O spells no,' said Mum, and sent him kicking and screaming next door. 'You can come home at five o'clock to get ready for Dave's party and not a minute before.'

Horrid Henry gazed longingly over the wall. His house looked so inviting. There was his bedroom window, twinkling at him. And his lonesome telly, stuck all by itself in the sitting room, just begging him to come over and switch it on. And all his wonderful toys, just waiting to be played with. Funny, thought Horrid Henry, his toys seemed so boring when he was in his room. But now that he was trapped at Margaret's, there was so much he longed to do at home.

Wait. He could hide out in his fort until five. Yes! Then he'd stroll into his house as if he'd been at Margaret's all day. But then Margaret's mum would be sure to call his mum to say that Henry had vanished and Henry would get into trouble. Big, big trouble. Big, big, banned from Dave's party trouble.

Or, he'd pretend to be sick. Margaret's mum was such an old fusspot she'd be sure to send him home immediately. Yippee. He was a genius. This would be easy. A few loud coughs, a few dramatic clutches at his stomach, a dash to the

loo, and he'd be sent straight home and . . . oops. He'd be put to bed. No party. No pizza. No bowling. And what was the point of pretending to be sick at the *weekend*? He was trapped.

Moody Margaret whacked her ruler on the table.

'I want everyone to write a story,' said Margaret.

Write a story! Boy would Horrid Henry write a story. He seized a piece of paper and a pencil and scribbled away.

'Who'd like to read their story to the class?' said Margaret.

'I will,' said Henry.

Once upon a time there was a moody old grouch named Margaret. Margaret had been born a frog but an ugly wizard cursed the frog and turned it into Margaret.

'That's enough, Henry,' snapped Margaret. Henry ignored her.

'Ribbet ribbet,' said Margaret Frog. 'Ribbet ribbet ribbet.' Everyone in the

kingdom tried to get rid of this horrible croaking moody monster. But she smelled so awful that no one could get near her. And then one day a hero named Heroic Henry came, and he held his nose, grabbed the Margaret Monster and hurled her into outer space where she exploded and was never seen again.

THE END

Susan giggled. Margaret glared.

'Fail,' said Margaret.

'Why?' said Horrid Henry innocently.

' 'Cause,' said Margaret. 'I'm the teacher and I say it was boring.'

'Did you think my story was boring, Peter?' demanded Henry.

Peter looked nervous.

'Did you?' said Margaret.

'Well, uhm, uhmm, I think mine is better,' said Peter.

Once upon a time there was a tea towel named Terry. He was a very sad tea towel because he didn't have any dishes

to dry. One day he found a lot of wet dishes. Swish swish swish, they were dry in no time. 'Yippee', said Terry the Tea Towel, 'I wonder when—'

'Boring!' shouted Horrid Henry.

'Excellent, Peter,' said Moody Margaret. '*Much* better than Henry's.'

Susan read out a story about her cat.

My cat Kitty Kat is a big fat cat. She says meow. One day Kitty Kat met a dog. Meow, said Kitty Kat. Woof woof, said the dog. Kitty Kat ran away. So did the dog. The end.

'OK class, here are your marks,' said Margaret. 'Peter came first.'

'Yay!' said Perfect Peter.

'*What*?' said Susan. 'My story was way better than his.'

'Susan came second, Henry came ninth.'

'How can I be ninth if there are only three people in the class?' demanded Horrid Henry.

' 'Cause that's how bad your story was,' said Margaret. 'Now, I've done some worksheets for you. No talking or there'll be no break.'

'Goody,' said Perfect Peter. 'I love worksheets. Are there lots of hard spelling words to learn?'

Horrid Henry had had enough. It was time to turn into Heroic Henry and destroy this horrible hag.

Henry crumpled up his worksheet and stood up.

'I've just been pretending to be a student,' shouted Henry. 'In fact, I'm a school inspector. And I'm shutting your school down. It's a disgrace.'

Margaret gasped.

'You're a moody old grouch and you're a terrible teacher,' said the inspector.

'I am not,' said Margaret.

'She is not,' said Susan.

'Silence when the inspector is speaking! You're the worst teacher I've ever seen. Imagine marking a stupid story about a tea towel higher than a fantastic tale about a wicked wizard.'

'I'm the head,' said Margaret. 'You can't boss me around.'

'I'm the inspector,' said Henry. 'I can boss *everyone* around.'

'Wrong, Henry,' said Margaret, 'because I'm the *chief* school inspector, and I'm inspecting *you*.'

'Oh no you're not,' said Henry.

'Oh yes I am,' said Margaret.

'An inspector can't be a head *and* a teacher, so there,' said Henry.

'Oh yes I can,' said Margaret.

'No you can't, 'cause I'm king and I send you to the Tower!' shrieked King Henry the Horrible.

'I'm the empress!' screamed Margaret. 'Go to jail.'

'I'm king of the universe, and I send you to the snakepit,' shrieked Henry.

'I'm queen of the universe and I'm going to chop off your head!'

'Not if I chop off yours first!' shrieked the king, yanking on the queen's hair.

The queen screamed and kicked the king.

The king screamed and kicked the queen.

'MUM!' screamed Margaret.

Margaret's mother rushed into the Secret Club tent.

'What's wrong with my little snugglechops?' said Margaret's mum.

'Henry's not playing my game,' said Margaret. 'And he kicked me.'

'She kicked me first,' said Henry.

'If you children can't play nicely I'll have to send you all home,' said Margaret's mother severely.

'No!' said Peter.

Send him . . . home. Yes! Henry would make Margaret scream until the walls fell down. He would tell Margaret's mum her house smelled of poo. He could . . . he would . . .

But if Henry was sent home for being horrid, Mum and Dad would be furious. There'd be no pizza and bowling party for sure.

Unless . . . unless . . . It was risky. It was dangerous. It could go horribly, horribly wrong. But desperate times call for desperate measures.

'Need a drink,' said Henry, and ran out of the tent before Margaret could stop him.

Henry went into the kitchen to find Margaret's mum.

'I'm worried about Margaret, I think she's getting sick,' said Henry.

'My little Maggie-muffin?' gasped Margaret's mum.

'She's being very strange,' said Henry sadly. 'She said she's the queen of the world and she would cut off my head.'

'Margaret would *never* say such a thing,' said her Mum. 'She always plays beautifully. I've never seen a child so good at sharing.'

Horrid Henry nodded. 'I know. It must be 'cause she's sick. Maybe she caught something from Peter.'

'Has Peter been ill?' said Margaret's mum. She looked pale.

'Oh yeah,' lied Henry. 'He's been throwing up, and—and—well, it's been awful. But I'm sure he's not *very* contagious.'

'Throwing up?' said Margaret's mum weakly.

'And diarrhoea,' said Henry. 'Loads and loads.'

Margaret's mother looked ashen.

'Diarrhoea?'

'But he's much better now,' said Henry. 'He's only run to the loo five times since we've been here.'

Margaret's mother looked faint. 'My little Margaret is so delicate . . . I can't risk . . .' she gasped. 'I think you and Peter had better go home straight away. Margaret! Margaret! Come in at once,' she shouted.

Horrid Henry did not wait to be told twice. School was out!

Ahhhh, thought Horrid Henry happily, reaching for the TV clicker, this was the life. Margaret had been sent to bed. He and Peter had been sent home. There was enough time to watch *Marvin the Maniac* and *Terminator Gladiator* before Dave's party.

'I can't help it that Margaret wasn't

feeling well, Mum,' said Horrid Henry. 'I just hope I haven't caught anything from *her*.'

Honestly.

Mum was so selfish.

The Purple Hand
Pirate Party

3

PERFECT PETER'S PIRATE PARTY

'Now, let's see,' said Mum, consulting her list, 'we need pirate flags, pieces of eight, swords, treasure chests, eyepatches, skull and crossbones plates. Have I missed anything?'

Horrid Henry stopped chewing. Wow! For once, Mum was talking about something important. His Purple Hand Pirate party wasn't till next month, but it was never too soon to start getting in supplies for the birthday party of the year. No, the century.

But wait. Mum had forgotten cutlasses. They were essential for the gigantic pirate battle Henry was planning. And what about all the ketchup for fake blood? And where were the buckets of sweets?

Horrid Henry opened his mouth to speak.

'That sounds great, Mum,' piped Perfect Peter. 'But don't forget the pirate napkins.'

'Napkins. Check,' said Mum, smiling.

Huh?

'I don't want napkins at my party,' said Horrid Henry.

'This isn't for your party,' said Mum. 'It's for Peter's.'

WHAT???

'What do you mean, it's for Peter's?' gasped Horrid Henry. He felt as if an icy hand had gripped him by the throat.

He was having trouble breathing.

'Peter's birthday is next week, and he's having a pirate party,' said Mum.

Perfect Peter kept eating his muesli.

'But he's having a Sammy the Snail party,' said Horrid Henry, glaring at Peter.

'I changed my mind,' said Perfect Peter.

'But pirates was *my* party idea!' shrieked Horrid Henry. 'I've been planning it for months. You're just a copycat.'

'You don't own pirates,' said Peter. 'Gordon had a pirate party for *his* birthday. So I want pirates for mine.'

'Henry, you can still have a pirate party,' said Dad.

'NOOOOOO!' screamed Horrid Henry. He couldn't have a pirate party *after* Peter. Everyone would think he'd copied his wormy toad brother.

Henry pounced. He was a poisoned arrow whizzing towards its target.

THUD! Peter fell off his chair.

SMASH! Peter's muesli bowl crashed to the floor.

'AAAEEEIIIII!' screeched Perfect Peter.

'Look what you've done, you horrid

boy!' yelled Mum. 'Say sorry to Peter.'

'WAAAAAAAAAAA!' sobbed Peter.

'I won't!' said Horrid Henry. 'I'm not sorry. He stole my party idea, and I hate him.'

'Then go to your room and stay there,' said Dad.

'It's not fair!' wailed Horrid Henry.

'What shall we do with the drunken sailor? What shall we do with the drunken sailor?' sang Perfect Peter as he walked past Henry's slammed bedroom door.

'Make him walk the plank!' screamed Horrid Henry. 'Which is what will happen to you if you don't SHUT UP!'

'Muum! Henry told me to shut up,' yelled Peter.

'Henry! Leave your brother alone,' said Mum.

'You're the eldest. Can't you be grown-up for once and let him have his party in peace?' said Dad.

NO! thought Horrid Henry. He could not. He had to stop Peter having a pirate party. He just had to.

But how?

He could bribe Peter. But that would cost money that Henry didn't have. He could promise to be nice to him . . . No way. That was going too far. That little copycat worm did not deserve Henry's niceness.

Maybe he could *trick* him into abandoning his party idea. Hmmmm. Henry smiled. Hmmmmm.

Horrid Henry opened Peter's bedroom door and sauntered in. Perfect Peter was busy writing names on his YO HO HO pirate invitations. The same ones, Henry noticed, that *he'd* been

planning to send, with the peg-legged pirate swirling his cutlass and looking like he was about to leap out at you.

'You're supposed to be in your room,' said Peter. 'I'm telling on you.'

'You know, Peter, I'm glad you're having a pirate party,' said Henry.

Peter paused.

'You are?' said Peter cautiously.

'Yeah,' said Horrid Henry. 'It means you'll get the pirate cannibal curse and I won't.'

'There's no such thing as a pirate cannibal curse,' said Peter.

'Fine,' said Horrid Henry. 'Just don't blame me when you end up as a shrunken head dangling round a cannibal's neck.'

Henry's such a liar, thought Peter. He's just trying to scare me.

'Gordon had a pirate party, and *he* didn't turn into a shrunken head,' said Peter.

Henry sighed.

'Of course not, because his name doesn't start with P. The cannibal pirate who made the curse was named Blood Boil Bob. Look, that's him on the invitations,' said Henry.

Peter glanced at the pirate. Was it his imagination, or did Blood Boil Bob have an especially mean and hungry look? Peter put down his crayon.

'He had a hateful younger brother named Paul, who became Blood Boil Bob's first shrunken head,' said Henry.

'Since then, the cannibal curse has passed down to anyone else whose name starts with P.'

'I don't believe you, Henry,' said Peter. He was sure Henry was trying to trick him. Lots of his friends had had pirate parties, and none of them had turned into a shrunken head.

On the other hand, none of his friends had names that began with P.

'How does the curse happen?' said Peter slowly.

Horrid Henry looked around. Then, putting a finger to his lips, he crept over to Peter's wardrobe and flung it open. Peter jumped.

'Just checking Blood Boil Bob's not in there,' whispered Henry. 'Now keep your voice down. Remember, dressing up as pirates, singing pirate songs, talking about treasure, wakes up the pirate cannibal. Sometimes — if you're lucky — he just steals all the treasure. Other times he . . . POUNCES,' shrieked Henry.

Peter turned pale.

'Yo ho, yo ho, a pirate's life for me,' sang Horrid Henry. 'Yo ho — whoops, sorry, better not sing, in case *he* turns up.'

'MUUUMMM!' wailed Peter. 'Henry's trying to scare me!'

'What's going on?' said Mum.

'Henry said I'm going to turn into a shrunken head if I have a pirate party.'

'Henry, don't be horrid,' said Mum, glaring. 'Peter, there's no such thing.'

'Told you, Henry,' said Perfect Peter.

'If I were you I'd have a Sammy the Slug party,' said Horrid Henry.

'Sammy the *Snail*,' said Peter. 'I'm having a pirate party and you can't stop me. So there.'

Rats, thought Horrid Henry. How could he make Peter change his mind?

'Don't **doooOOO IT**, Peter,' Henry howled spookily under Peter's door every night. 'Beware! Beware!'

'Stop it, Henry!' screamed Peter.

'You'll be sorry,' Horrid Henry

scrawled all over Peter's homework.

'Remember the cannibal curse,' Henry whispered over supper the night before the party.

'Henry, leave your brother alone or you won't be coming to the party,' said Mum.

What? Miss out on chocolate pieces of eight? Henry scowled. That was the least he was owed.

It was so unfair. Why did Peter have to wreck everything?

*

It was Peter's birthday party. Mum and Dad hung two huge skull and crossbones pirate flags outside the house. The exact ones, Horrid Henry noted bitterly, that he had planned for *his* birthday party. The cutlasses had been decorated and the galleon cake eaten. All that remained was for Peter's horrible guests, Tidy Ted, Spotless Sam, Goody-Goody Gordon, Perky Parveen, Helpful Hari, Tell-Tale Tim and Mini Minnie to go on the treasure hunt.

'Yo ho, yo ho, a pirate's life for me,' sang Horrid Henry. He was wearing his pirate skull scarf, his eyepatch, and his huge black skull and crossbones hat. His bloody cutlass gleamed.

'Don't sing that,' said Peter.

'Why not, baby?' said Henry.

'You know why,' muttered Peter.

'I warned you about Blood Boil Bob, but you wouldn't listen,' hissed Henry, 'and now—' he drew his hand across his throat. 'Hey everyone, let's play pin the tail on Peter.'

'MUUUUUUUUUMMMMMMM!' wailed Peter.

'Behave yourself, Henry,' muttered Mum, 'or you won't be coming on the treasure hunt.'

Henry scowled. The only reason he was even at this baby party was because the treasure chest was filled with chocolate pieces of eight.

Mum clapped her hands.

'Come on everyone, look for the clues hidden around the house to help you find the pirate treasure,' she said, handing Peter a scroll. 'Here's the first one.'

Climb the stair,
if you dare,
you'll find a clue,
just for you.

'I found a clue,' squealed Helpful Hari, grabbing the scroll dangling from the banister.

'Turn to the left,
turn to the right,
reach into the bag,
don't get a fright.'

The party pounded off to the left, then to the right, where another scroll hung in a pouch from Peter's doorknob.

'I found the treasure map!' shouted Perky Parveen.

'Oh goody,' said Goody-Goody Gordon.

Everyone gathered round the ancient scroll.

'It says to go to the park,' squealed Spotless Sam. 'Look, X marks the spot where the treasure is buried.'

Dad, waving a skull and crossbones flag, led the pirates out of the door and down the road to the park.

Horrid Henry ran ahead through the

park gates and took off his skull and crossbones hat and eyepatch. No way did he want anyone to think he was part of this *baby* pirate party. He glanced at the swings. Was there anyone here that he knew? Phew, no one, just some little girl on the slide.

The little girl looked up and stared at Horrid Henry. Horrid Henry stared back.

Uh oh.

Oh no.

Henry began to back away. But it was too late.

'Henwy!' squealed the little girl. 'Henwy!'

It was Lisping Lily, New Nick's horrible sister. Henry had met her on the world's worst sleepover at Nick's house, where she—where she—

'Henwy! I love you, Henwy!' squealed

Lisping Lily, running towards him. 'Will you marry with me, Henwy?'

Horrid Henry turned and ran down the windy path into the gardens. Lisping Lily ran after him. 'Henwy! Henwy!'

Henry dived into some thick bushes and crouched behind them.

Please don't find me, please don't find me, he prayed.

Henry waited, his heart pounding. All he could hear was Peter's pirate party, advancing his way. Had he lost her?

'I think the treasure's over there!' shouted Peter.

Phew. He'd ditched her. He was safe.

'Henwy?' came a little voice. 'Henwy! Where are you? I want to give you a big kiss.'

AAAARRRGGHH!

Then Horrid Henry remembered who he was. The boy who'd got Miss

Battle-Axe sent to the head. The boy who'd defeated the demon dinner lady. The boy who was scared of nothing (except injections). What was a pirate king like him doing hiding from some tiddly toddler?

Horrid Henry put on his pirate hat and grabbed his cutlass. He'd scare her off if it was the last thing he did.

'AAAAARRRRRRRRRRR!' roared the pirate king, leaping up and brandishing his bloody cutlass.

'AAAAAAAAAAAHHH!' squealed Lisping Lily. She turned and ran, crashing into Peter.

'Piwates! Piwates!' she screamed, dashing away.

Perfect Peter's blood ran cold. He looked into the thrashing bushes and saw a skull and crossbones rising out of the hedge, the gleam of sunlight on a

blood-red cutlass…

'AAAAAAAHHHHHH!' screamed Peter. 'It's Blood Boil Bob!' He turned and ran.

'AAAAAAAHHHHHH!' shrieked Ted. He turned and ran.

'AAAAAAAHHHHHH!' shrieked Gordon, Parveen, and the rest. They turned and ran.

Huh? thought Horrid Henry, trying to wriggle free.

Thud.

Henry's foot knocked against something hard. There, hidden beneath some leaves under the hedge, was a pirate chest.

Eureka!

'Help!' shrieked Perfect Peter. 'Help! Help!'

Mum and Dad ran over.

'What's happened?'

'We got attacked by pirates!' wailed

Parveen.

'We ran for our lives!' wailed Gordon.

'Pirates?' said Mum.

'Pirates?' said Dad. 'How many were there?'

'Five!'

'Ten!'

'Hundreds!' wailed Mini Minnie.

'Don't be silly,' said Mum.

'I'm sure they're gone now, so let's find the treasure,' said Dad.

Peter opened the map and headed for the hedge nearest to the gate where the treasure map showed a giant X.

'I'm too scared,' he whimpered.

Helpful Hari crept to the treasure chest and lifted the lid. Everyone gasped. All that was left inside were a few crumpled gold wrappers.

'The treasure's gone,' whispered Peter.

Just then Horrid Henry sauntered along the path, twirling his hat.

'Where have you been?' said Mum.

'Hiding,' said Horrid Henry truthfully.

'We got raided,' gasped Ted.

'By pirates,' gasped Gordon.

'No way,' said Horrid Henry.

'They stole all the pieces of eight,' wailed Peter.

Horrid Henry sighed.

'What did I tell you about the cannibal curse?' he said. 'Just be glad you've still got your heads.'

Hmmmm, boy, chocolate pieces of eight were always yummy, but raided pieces of eight tasted even better, thought Horrid Henry that night, shoving a few more chocolates into his mouth.

Come to think of it, there'd been too many pirate parties recently.

Now, a cannibal curse party . . . Hmmmn.

GOTCHA

why did she have to play at his house? Why couldn't her mum just dump her in the bin where she belonged?

Unfortunately, the last time they'd played *Gotcha*, Margaret had won. The last two, three, four and five times they'd played, Margaret had won. Margaret was a demon *Gotcha* player.

Well, not any longer.

This time, Henry was determined to beat her. Horrid Henry hated losing. By hook or by crook, he would triumph. Moody Margaret had beaten him at *Gotcha* for the very last time.

'Who'll be banker?' said Perfect Peter.

'Me,' said Margaret.

'Me,' said Henry. Being in charge of all the game's treasure was an excellent way of topping up your coffers when none of the other players was looking.

'I'm the guest so *I'm* banker,' said Margaret. 'You can be the dragon keeper.'

Horrid Henry's hand itched to yank Margaret's hair. But then Margaret would scream and scream and Mum would send Henry to his room and

'Muuum! Henry's cheating!' shrieked Peter.

'If I get called one more time,' screamed Mum from upstairs, 'I will throw that game in the bin.'

Eeeek.

Margaret rolled. Three.

'You breathed on me,' hissed Margaret.

'Did not,' said Henry.

'Did too,' said Margaret. 'I get another go.'

'No way,' said Henry.

Peter picked up the dice.

'Low roll, low roll, low roll,' chanted Henry.

'Stop it, Henry,' said Peter.

'Low roll, low roll, low roll,' chanted

Henry louder.

Peter rolled an eleven.

'Yippee, I go first,' trilled Peter.

Henry glared at him.

Perfect Peter took a deep breath, and rolled the dice to start the game.

Five. A Fate square.

Perfect Peter moved his gargoyle to the Fate square and picked up a Fate card. Would it tell him to claim a treasure hoard, or send him to the Dungeon? He squinted at it.

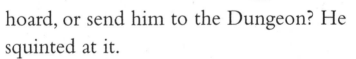

'The og . . . the ogr . . . I can't read it,' he said. 'The words are too hard for me.'

Henry snatched the card. It read:

The Ogres make you king for a day. Collect 20 rubies from the other players.

'The Ogres make you king for a day. Give 20 rubies to the player on your left,' read Henry. 'And that's me, so pay up.'

Perfect Peter handed Henry twenty rubies.

Tee hee, thought Horrid Henry.

'I think you read that Fate card wrong, Henry,' said Moody Margaret grimly.

Uh oh. If Margaret read Peter the card, he was dead. Mum would make them stop playing, and Henry would get into trouble. Big, big trouble.

'Didn't,' said Henry.

'Did,' said Margaret. 'I'm telling on you.'

Horrid Henry looked at the card again. 'Whoops. Silly me. I read it too fast,' said Henry. 'It says, give 20 rubies to *all* the other players.'

'Thought so,' said Moody Margaret.

Perfect Peter rolled the dice. Nine! Oh no, that took Peter straight to Eerie

Eyrie, Henry's favourite lair. Now Peter could buy it. Everyone always landed on it and had to pay ransom or get eaten. Rats, rats, rats.

'1, 2, 3, 4, 5, 6, 7, 8, 9, look, Henry, I've landed on Eerie Eyrie and no one owns it yet,' said Peter.

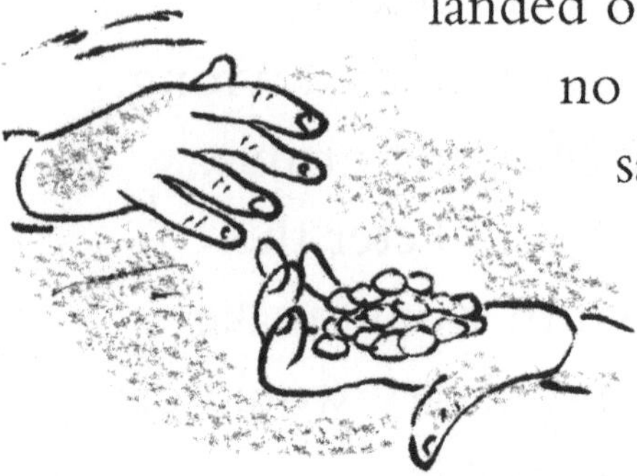

'Don't buy it,' said Henry. 'It's the worst lair on the board. No one ever lands on it. You'd just be wasting your money.'

'Oh,' said Peter. He looked doubtful.

'But . . . but . . .' said Peter.

'Save your money for when you land in other people's lairs,' said Henry. 'That's what I'd do.'

'OK,' said Peter, 'I'm not buying.'

Tee hee.

Henry rolled. Six. Yes! He landed on Eerie Eyrie. 'I'm buying it!' crowed Henry.

'But Henry,' said Peter, 'you just told me not to buy it.'

'You shouldn't listen to me,' said Henry.

'MUM!' wailed Peter.

Soon Henry owned Eerie Eyrie, Gryphon Gulch and Creepy Hollow, but he was dangerously low on treasure. Margaret owned Rocky Ravine, Vulture Valley, and Hideous Hellmouth. Margaret kept her treasure in her treasure pouch, so it was impossible to see how much money she had, but Henry guessed she was also low.

Peter owned Demon Den and one dragon egg.

Margaret was stuck in the Dungeon. Yippee! This meant if Henry landed on one of her lairs he'd be safe. Horrid Henry rolled, and landed on Vulture Valley, guarded by a baby dragon.

'Gotcha!' shrieked Margaret. 'Gimme 25 rubies.'

'You're in the Dungeon, you can't collect ransom,' said Henry. 'Nah nah ne nah nah!'

'Can!'

'Can't!'

'That's how we play in *my* house,' said Margaret.

'In case you hadn't noticed, we're not *at* your house,' said Henry.

'But I'm the guest,' said Margaret. 'Gimme my money!'

'No!' shouted Henry. 'You can't just make up rules.'

'The rules say . . .' began Perfect Peter.

'Shut up, Peter!' screamed Henry and Margaret.

'I'm not paying,' said Henry.

Margaret glowered. 'I'll get you for this, Henry,' she hissed.

It was Peter's turn. Henry had just upgraded his baby dragon guarding Eerie Eyrie to a big, huge, fire-breathing, slavering monster dragon. Peter was only

five squares away. If Peter landed there, he'd be out of the game.

'Land! Land! Land! Land! Land!' chanted Henry. 'Yum yum yum, my dragon is just waiting to eat you up.'

'Stop it, Henry,' said Peter. He rolled. Five.

'Gotcha!' shouted Horrid Henry. 'I own Eerie Eyrie! You've landed in my lair, pay up! That's 100 rubies.'

'I don't have enough money,' wailed Perfect Peter.

Horrid Henry drew his finger

across his throat.

'You're dead meat, worm,' he chortled.

Perfect Peter burst into tears and ran out of the room.

'Waaaaaaahhhhh,' he wailed. 'I lost!'

Horrid Henry glared at Moody Margaret.

Moody Margaret glared at Horrid Henry.

'You're next to be eaten,' snarled Margaret.

'*You're* next,' snarled Henry.

Henry peeked under the *Gotcha* board where his treasure was hidden. Oh no. Not again. He'd spent so much on dragons he was down to his last few rubies. If he landed on any of Margaret's lairs, he'd be wiped out. He had to get more treasure. He had to. Why oh why had he let Margaret be banker?

His situation was desperate. Peter was easy to steal money from, but Margaret's eagle eyes never missed a trick. What to do, what to do? He had to get more treasure, he had to.

And then suddenly Horrid Henry had a brilliant, spectacular idea. It was so brilliant that Henry couldn't believe he'd never thought of it before. It was dangerous. It was risky. But what choice did he have?

'I need the loo,' said Henry.

'Hurry up,' said Margaret, scowling.

Horrid Henry dashed to the downstairs loo . . . and sneaked straight out of the back door. Then he jumped over the garden wall and crept into Margaret's house.

Quickly he ran to her sitting room

and scanned her games cupboard. Aha! There was Margaret's *Gotcha*.

Horrid Henry stuffed his pockets with treasure. He stuffed more under his shirt and in his socks.

'Is that you, my little sugarplum?' came a voice from upstairs. 'Maggie Moo-Moo?'

Henry froze. Margaret's mum was home.

'Maggie Plumpykins,' cooed her mum, coming down the stairs. 'Is that you–oooo?'

'No,' squeaked Henry. 'I mean, yes,' he

squawked. 'Got to go back to Henry's, 'bye!'

And Horrid Henry ran for his life.

'You took a long time,' said Margaret.

Henry hugged his stomach.

'Upset tummy,' he lied. Oh boy was he brilliant. Now, with loads of cash which he would slip under the board, he was sure to win.

Henry picked up the dice and handed them to Margaret.

'Your turn,' said Henry.

Henry's hungry dragon stood waiting six places away in Goblin Gorge.

Roll a six, roll a six, roll a six, prayed Horrid Henry.

Not a six, not a six, not a six, prayed Moody Margaret.

Margaret rolled. Four. She moved her skull to the Haunted Forest.

'Your turn,' said Margaret.

Henry rolled a three. Oh no. He'd landed on Hideous Hellmouth, where Margaret's giant dragon loomed.

'Yes!' squealed Margaret. 'Gotcha! You're dead! Ha ha hahaha, I won!' Moody Margaret leapt to her feet and did a victory dance, whooping and cheering.

Horrid Henry smiled at her.

'Oh dear,' said Horrid Henry. 'Oh dearie, dearie me. Looks like I'm dragon food — NOT!'

'What do you mean, not?' said

Margaret. 'You're dead meat, you can't pay me.'

'Not so fast,' said Horrid Henry. With a flourish he reached under the board and pulled out a wodge of treasure.

'Let me see, 100 rubies, is it?' said Henry, counting off a pile of coins.

Margaret's mouth dropped open.

'How did you . . . what . . . how . . . huh?' she spluttered.

Henry shrugged modestly. 'Some of us know how to play this game,' he said. 'Now roll.'

Moody Margaret rolled and landed on

a Fate square.

Go straight to Eerie Eyrie, read the card.

'Gotcha!' shrieked Horrid Henry. He'd won!! Margaret didn't have enough money to stop being eaten. She was dead. She was doomed.

'I won! I won! You can't pay me, nah nah ne nah nah,' shrieked Horrid Henry, leaping up and doing a victory dance. 'I am the *Gotcha* king!'

'Says who?' said Moody Margaret, pulling a handful of treasure from her pouch.

Huh?

'You stole that money!' spluttered Henry. 'You stole the bank's money. You big fat cheater.'

'Didn't.'

'Did.'

'CHEATER!' howled Moody Margaret.

'CHEATER!' howled Horrid Henry.

Moody Margaret grabbed the board and hurled it to the floor.

'I won,' said Horrid Henry.

'Did not.'

'Did too, Maggie Moo-Moo.'

'Don't call me that,' said Margaret, glaring.

'Call you what, Moo-Moo?'

'I challenge you to a re-match,' said Moody Margaret.

'You're on,' said Horrid Henry.

HORRID HENRY
Wakes the Dead

For Steven Butler
the original Horrid Henry

CONTENTS

1

HORRID HENRY AND THE TV REMOTE

Horrid Henry pushed through the front door. Perfect Peter squeezed past him and ran inside.

'Hey!' screamed Horrid Henry, dashing after him. 'Get back here, worm.'

'Noooo!' squealed Perfect Peter, running as fast as his little legs would carry him.

Henry grabbed Peter's shirt, then hurtled past him into the sitting room. Yippee! He was going to get the comfy black chair first. Almost there, almost there, almost . . . and then Horrid Henry skidded on a sock and slipped. Peter pounded past and dived onto the comfy black chair. Panting and gasping, he snatched the remote control. Click!

'All together now! Who's a silly Billy?' trilled the world's most annoying goat.

'Billy!' sang out Perfect Peter.

NOOOOOOOOOOOOO!

It had happened again. Just as Henry was looking forward to resting his weary bones on the comfy black chair after another long, hard, terrible day at school and watching *Rapper Zapper* and *Knight Fight*, Peter had somehow managed to nab the chair first. It was so unfair.

The rule in Henry's house was that whoever was sitting in the comfy black chair decided what to watch on TV. And there was Peter, smiling and singing along with Silly Billy, the revolting singing goat who thought he was a clown.

Henry's parents were so mean and horrible, they only had one teeny tiny telly in the whole, entire house. It was so minuscule Henry practically had to watch it using a magnifying glass. And so old you practically had to kick it

to turn it on. Everyone else he knew had loads of TVs. Rude Ralph had five ginormous ones all to himself. At least, that's what Ralph said.

All too often there were at least two great programmes on at the same time. How was Henry supposed to choose between *Mutant Max* and *Terminator Gladiator*? If only he could watch two TVs simultaneously, wouldn't life be wonderful?

Even worse, Mum, Dad, and Peter had their own smelly programmes *they* wanted to watch. And not great programmes like *Hog House* and *Gross Out*. Oh no. Mum and Dad liked watching . . . news. Documentaries. Opera. Perfect Peter liked nature programmes. And revolting baby programmes like *Daffy and her Dancing Daisies*. Uggghh! How did he end up in this family? When would his real parents, the King and Queen, come and fetch him and take him to the palace where he could watch whatever he wanted all day?

When he grew up and became King Henry the Horrible, he'd have three TVs in every room, including the bathrooms.

But until that happy day, he was stuck at home slugging it out with Peter. He *could* spend the afternoon watching *Silly Billy*, *Cooking Cuties*, and *Sammy the Snail*. Or . . .

Horrid Henry pounced and snatched the remote. CLICK!

'. . . and the black knight lowers his visor . . .'

'Give it to me,' shrieked Peter.

'No,' said Henry.

'But I've got the chair,' wailed Peter.

'So?' said Henry, waving the clicker at him. 'If you want the remote you'll have to come and get it.'

Peter hesitated. Henry dangled the remote just out of reach.

Perfect Peter slipped off the comfy black chair and grabbed for the remote. Horrid Henry ducked, swerved and jumped onto the empty chair.

'. . . And the knights are advancing towards one another, lances poised . . .'

'MUUUUMMMM!' squealed Peter. 'Henry snatched the remote!'

'Did not!'

'Did too.'

'Did not, wibble pants.'

'Don't call me wibble pants,' cried Peter.

'Okay, pongy poo poo,' said Henry.

'Don't call me pongy poo poo,' shrieked Peter.

'Okay, wibble bibble,' said Horrid Henry.

'MUUUUUMMMM!' wailed Peter. 'Henry's calling me names!'

'Henry! Stop being horrid,' shouted Mum.

'I'm just trying to watch TV in peace!' screamed Henry. 'Peter's annoying me.'

'Henry's annoying *me*,' whined Peter. 'He pushed me off the chair.'

'Liar,' said Henry. 'You fell off.'

'MUUUUMMMMMM!' screamed Peter.

Mum ran in, and grabbed the remote.

Click! The screen went black.

'I've had it with you boys fighting over the TV,' shouted Mum. 'No TV for the rest of the day.'

What?

Huh?

'But . . . but . . .' said Perfect Peter.

'But . . . but . . .' said Horrid Henry.

'No buts,' said Mum.

'It's not fair!' wailed Henry and Peter.

Horrid Henry paced up and down his room, whacking his teddy, Mr Kill, on the bedpost every time he walked past.

WHACK!

WHACK!

WHACK!

He had to find a way to make sure he watched the programmes *he* wanted to watch. He just had to. He'd have to get up at the crack of dawn. There was no other way.

Unless . . .

Unless . . .

And then Horrid Henry had a brilliant, spectacular idea. What an idiot he'd been. All those months he'd missed his fantastic shows . . . Well, never ever again.

Sneak.

Sneak.

Sneak.

It was the middle of the night. Horrid Henry crept down the stairs as quietly as he could and tiptoed into the sitting room, shutting the door behind him. There was the TV, grumbling in the corner. 'Why is no one watching me?' moaned the telly. 'C'mon, Henry.'

But for once Henry didn't listen. He had something much more important to do.

He crept to the comfy black chair and fumbled in the dark. Now, where was the remote? Aha! There it was. As usual, it had fallen between the seat cushion and the armrest. Henry grabbed it. Quick as a flash, he switched the TV over to the channel for *Rapper Zapper*, *Talent Tigers* and *Hog House*. Then he tiptoed to the toy cupboard and hid the remote control deep inside a bucket of multi-coloured bricks that no one had played with for years.

Tee hee, thought Horrid Henry.

Why should he have to get up to grab the comfy black chair hours before his programmes started when he could have a lovely lie-in, saunter downstairs whenever he felt like it, and be master of the TV? Whoever was sitting in the chair could be in charge of the telly all they wanted. But without the TV remote, no one would be watching anything.

Perfect Peter stretched out on the comfy black chair. Hurrah. Serve Henry right for being so mean to him. Peter had got downstairs first. Now he could watch what *he* wanted all morning.

Peter reached for the remote control. It wasn't on the armrest. It wasn't on the headrest. Had it slipped between the armrest and the cushion? No. He felt round the back. No. He looked under the chair. Nothing. He looked behind the chair. Where was it?

Horrid Henry strolled into the sitting room. Peter clutched tightly onto the armrests in case Henry tried to push him off.

'I got the comfy black chair first,' said Peter.

'Okay,' said Horrid Henry, sitting down on the sofa. 'So let's watch something.'

Peter looked at Henry suspiciously.

'Where's the remote?' said Peter.

'I dunno,' said Horrid Henry. 'Where did you put it?'

'I didn't put it anywhere,' said Peter.

'You had it last,' said Henry.

'No I didn't,' said Peter.

'Did,' said Henry.

'Didn't,' said Peter.

Perfect Peter sat on the comfy black chair. Horrid Henry sat on the sofa.

'Have you seen it anywhere?' said Peter.

'No,' said Henry. 'You'll just have to look for it, won't you?'

Peter eyed Henry warily.

'I'm waiting,' said Horrid Henry.

Perfect Peter didn't know what to do. If he got up from the chair to look for the remote Henry would jump into it and there was no way Henry would decide to watch *Cooking Cuties*, even though today they were showing how to make your own muesli.

On the other hand, there wasn't much point sitting in the chair if he didn't have the remote.

Henry sat.

Peter sat.

'You know, Peter, you can turn on the TV without the remote,' said Henry casually.

Peter brightened. 'You can?'

'Sure," said Henry. 'You just press that big black button on the left."

Peter stared suspiciously at the button.

Henry must think he was an idiot. He could see Henry's plan from miles away. The moment Peter left the comfy black chair Henry would jump on it.

'You press it,' said Peter.

'Okay," said Henry agreeably. He sauntered to the telly and pressed the 'on' button.

BOOM! CRASH! WALLOP!

'Des-troy! Des-troy!' bellowed Mutant Max.

'Go Mutants!' shouted Horrid Henry, bouncing up and down.

Perfect Peter sat frozen in the chair.

'But I want to watch *Sing-along with Susie!*' wailed Peter. 'She's teaching a song about raindrops and roses.'

'So find the remote,' said Horrid Henry.

'I can't,' said Peter.

'Tough,' said Horrid Henry. 'Pulverize! Destroy! Destroy!'

Tee hee.

What a fantastic day, sighed Horrid Henry happily. He'd watched every single one of *his* best programmes and Peter hadn't watched a single one of *his*. And now *Hog House* was on. Could life get any better?

Dad staggered into the sitting room. 'Ahh, a little relaxation in front of the telly,' sighed Dad. 'Henry, turn off that horrible programme. I want to watch the news.'

'Shhh!' said Horrid Henry. How dare Dad interrupt him?

'Henry . . .' said Dad.

'I can't,' said Horrid Henry. 'No remote.'

'What do you mean, no remote?' said Dad.

'It's gone,' said Henry.

'What do you mean, gone?' said Mum.

'Henry lost it,' said Peter.

'Didn't,' snapped Henry.

'Did,' said Peter.

'DIDN'T!' bellowed Henry. 'Now be quiet, I'm trying to watch.'

Mum marched over to the telly and switched it off.

'The TV stays off un[illegible] remote is found,' said Mum.

'But I didn't lose it!' [illegible] Peter.

'Neither did I,' said Horrid Henry. This wasn't a lie, as he *hadn't* lost it.

Rats. Maybe it was time for the TV remote to make a miraculous return . . .

Sneak.

Sneak.

Sneak.

Mum and Dad were in the kitchen. Perfect Peter was practising his cello.

Horrid Henry crept to the toy cupboard and opened it.

The bucket of bricks had gone.

Huh?

Henry searched frantically in the cupboard, hurling out jigsaw puzzles, board games, and half-empty paint bottles. The bricks were definitely gone.

Yikes. Horrid Henry felt a chill down his spine. He was dead. He was doomed.

Unless Mum [illegible] moved the bricks

somewhere. Of course. Phew. He wasn't dead yet.

Mum walked into the sitting room.

'Mum,' said Henry casually, 'I wanted to build a castle with those old bricks but when I went to get them from the cupboard they'd gone.'

Mum stared at him. 'You haven't played with those bricks in years, Henry. I had a good clear out of all the baby toys today and gave them to the charity shop.'

Charity shop? Charity shop? That meant the remote was gone for good.

He would be in trouble. Big big trouble. He was doomed . . . NOT!

Without the clicker, the TV would be useless. Mum and Dad would *have* to buy a new one. Yes! A bigger, better fantastic one with twenty-five surround-sound speakers and a mega-whopper 10-foot super-sized screen!

'You know, Mum, we wouldn't have any arguments if we all had our *own* TVs,' said Henry. Yes! In fact, if he had two in his bedroom, and a third one spare in case one of them ever broke, he'd never argue about the telly again.

Mum sighed. 'Just find the remote,' she said. 'It must be here somewhere.'

'But our TV is so old,' said Henry.

'It's fine,' said Dad.

'It's horrible,' said Henry.

'We'll see,' said Mum.

New TV here I come, thought Horrid Henry happily.

Mum sat down on the sofa and opened her book.

Dad sat down on the sofa and opened his book.

Peter sat down on the sofa and opened his book.

'You know,' said Mum, 'it's lovely and peaceful without the telly.'

'Yes,' said Dad.

'No squabbling,' said Mum.

'No screaming,' said Dad.

'Loads of time to read good books,' said Mum.

They smiled at each other.

'I think we should be a telly-free home from now on,' said Dad.

'Me too,' said Mum.

'That's a great idea,' said Perfect Peter. 'More time to do homework.'

'What??" screamed Horrid Henry. He thought his heart would stop. No TV? No TV? 'NOOOOOOOOOOO! NOOOOOOOOOOO! NOOOOOOOOOOO!'

BANG! ZAP! KER-POW!

'Go mutants!' yelped Horrid Henry, bouncing up and down in the comfy black chair.

Mum and Dad had resisted buying a new telly for two long hard horrible weeks. Finally they'd given in. Of course they hadn't bought a big mega-whopper super-duper telly. Oh no. They'd bought the teeniest, tiniest, titchiest telly they could.

Still. It was a *bit* bigger than the old one. And the remote could always go missing again . . .

2

HORRID HENRY'S SCHOOL ELECTION

Yack yack yack yack yack.

Horrid Henry's legs ached. His head ached. His bottom really ached. How much longer would he have to sit on this hard wooden floor and listen to Mrs Oddbod witter on about hanging up coats and no running in the corridors and walking down staircases on the right-hand side? Why were school assemblies so boring? If he were head, assemblies would be about the best TV programmes, competitions for gruesome grub recipes and speed-eating contests.

Yack. Yack. Yack. Yack. Yack.

Zoom . . . Zoom . . . Squawk! Horrid Henry's hawk swooped and scooped up Mrs Oddbod in his fearsome beak.

Chomp.

Chomp.

Ch– Wait a minute. What was she saying?

'School elections will be held next week,' said Mrs Oddbod. 'For the first time ever you'll be electing a School Council President. Now I want everyone to think of someone they believe would make an outstanding President. Someone who will make important decisions which will affect everyone, someone worthy of this high office, someone who will represent this school . . .'

Horrid Henry snorted. School elections? Phooey! Who'd want to be School Council President? All that responsibility . . . all that power . . . all that glory . . . Wait. What was he thinking? Who *wouldn't* want to be?

Imagine, being President! He'd be king, emperor, Lord High Master of the Universe! He'd make Mrs Oddbod walk the plank. He'd send Miss Battle-Axe to be a galley slave. He'd make playtime last for five hours. He'd ban all salad and vegetables from school dinners and just serve sweets! And Fizzywizz drinks! And everyone would have to bow down to him as they entered the school! And give him chocolate every day.

President Henry. His Honour, President Henry. It had a nice ring. So did King Henry. Emperor Henry would be even better though. He'd change his title as soon as he got the throne.

And all he had to do was win the election.

Shout!

Shriek!

'Silence!' screeched Mrs Oddbod. 'Any more noise and playtime will be cancelled!'

Huumph, that was one thing that would never happen when he was School President. In fact, he'd make it a rule that anyone who put their hand up in class would get sent to him for punishment. There'd only be shouting out in *his* school.

'Put up your hand if you wish to nominate someone,' said Mrs Oddbod.

Sour Susan's hand shot up. 'I nominate Margaret,' she said.

'I accept!' yelled Margaret, preening.

Horrid Henry choked. Margaret? Bossyboots Margaret *President*? She'd be a disaster, a horrible, grumpy, grouchy, moody disaster. Henry would never hear the end of it. Her head would swell so much it would burst. She'd be swaggering all over the place, ordering everyone around, boasting, bossing, showing off . . .

Horrid Henry's hand shot up. 'I nominate . . . me!' he shrieked.

'You?' said Mrs Oddbod coldly.

'Me,' said Horrid Henry.

'I second it,' shouted Rude Ralph.

Henry beamed at Ralph. He'd make Ralph his Grand Vizier. Or maybe Lord High Executioner.

'Any more nominations?' said Mrs Oddbod. She looked unhappy. 'Come on, Bert, what would you do to improve the school?'

'I dunno,' said Bert.

'Clare?' said Mrs Oddbod.

'More fractions!' said Clare.

Horrid Henry caught Ralph's eye.

'Boo!' yelled Ralph. 'Down with Clare!'

'Yeah, boo!' yelled Dizzy Dave.

'Boo!' hissed Horrid Henry.

'Last chance to nominate anyone else,' said Mrs Oddbod desperately.

Silence.

'All right,' said Mrs Oddbod, 'you have two candidates for President. Posters can be displayed from tomorrow. Speeches the day after tomorrow. Good luck to both candidates.'

Horrid Henry glared at Moody Margaret.

Moody Margaret glared at Horrid Henry.

I'll beat that grumpface frog if it's the last thing I do, thought Horrid Henry.

I'll beat that pongy pants pimple if it's the last thing I do, thought Moody Margaret.

'Vote Margaret! Margaret for President!' trilled Sour Susan the next day, as she and Margaret handed out leaflets during playtime.

'Ha ha Henry, I'm going to win, and you're not!' chanted Margaret, sticking out her tongue.

'Yeah Henry, Margaret's going to win,' said Sour Susan.

'Oh yeah?' said Henry. Wait till she saw his fantastic campaign posters with the big picture of King Henry the Horrible.

'Yeah.'

'We'll see about that,' said Horrid Henry.

He'd better start campaigning at once. Now, whose votes could he count on?

Ralph's for sure. And, uh . . . um . . . uhmmmm . . . Ralph.

Toby *might* vote for him but he'd probably have to beg. Hmmm. Two votes were not enough to win. He'd have to get more support. Well, no time like the present to remind everyone what a great guy he was.

Zippy Zoe zipped past. Horrid Henry smiled at her. Zoe stopped dead.

'Why are you smiling at me, Henry?' said Zippy Zoe. She checked to see if she'd come to school wearing pyjamas or if her jumper had a big hole.

'Just because it's so nice to see you,'

said Horrid Henry. 'Will you vote for me for President?'

Zoe stared at him. 'Margaret gave me a pencil with her name on it,' said Zoe. 'And a sticker. What will *you* give me?'

Give? Give? Horrid Henry liked getting. He did not like giving. So Margaret was bribing people, was she? Well, two could play at that game. He'd bring loads of sweets into school tomorrow and hand them out to everyone who promised to vote for him. That would guarantee victory! And he'd make sure that everyone had to give *him* sweets after he'd won.

Anxious Andrew walked by wearing a 'Margaret for President' sticker.

'Oooh, Andrew, I wouldn't vote for her,' said Henry. 'Do you know what she's planning to do?' Henry whispered in Andrew's ear. Andrew gasped.

'No,' said Andrew.

'Yes,' said Henry. 'And ban crisps, too. You know what an old bossyboots Margaret is.'

Henry handed him a leaflet.

Andrew looked uncertain.

'Vote for me and I'll make you Vice-Chairman of the Presidential Snacks Sub-committee.'

'Oooh,' said Andrew.

Henry promised the same job to Dizzy Dave, Jolly Josh, and Weepy William.

He promised Needy Neil his mum could sit with him in class. He promised Singing Soraya she could sing every day in assembly. He promised Greedy Graham there'd be ice cream every day for lunch.

The election is in the bag, thought Horrid Henry gleefully. He fingered the magic marker in his pocket. Tee hee. Just wait till Margaret saw how he was planning to graffiti her poster! And wasn't it lucky it was impossible to graffiti *his* name or change it to something rude. Shame, thought Horrid Henry, that Peter wasn't running for President. If you crossed out the 't' and the 'r' you'd get 'Vote for Pee'.

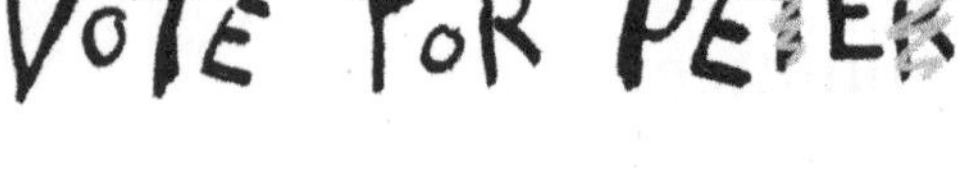

Horrid Henry strolled over to the wall where the campaign posters were displayed.

Huh?

What?

A terrible sight met his eyes. His 'Vote for Henry' posters had been defaced. Instead of his crowned head, a horrible picture of a chicken's head had been glued on top of his body. And the 'ry' of his name had been crossed out.

Beneath it was written:

Cluck cluck yuck! Vote for a Hen? No way!

What a dirty trick, thought Horrid Henry indignantly.

How dare Margaret deface his posters! Just because he'd handed out leaflets showing Margaret with a frog's face. Margaret *was* a frog-face. The school needed to know the truth about her.

Well, no more Mr Nice Guy. This was war.

Moody Margaret entered the playground. A terrible sight met her eyes. All her 'Vote Margaret' posters had been defaced. Huge beards and moustaches had been drawn on every one. Beneath the picture, instead of 'Be on target! Vote Margaret!' the words now read:

Be on Target
Vote Margaret

The next poster read:

How dare Henry graffiti over her posters! I'll get you Henry, thought Margaret. Just wait until tomorrow.

The next day was campaign speech day. Horrid Henry sat on the stage with Moody Margaret in front of the entire school. He was armed and ready. Margaret would be blasted from the race. As Margaret rose to speak, Henry made a horrible, gagging face.

'We face a great danger,' said Moody Margaret. 'Do you want a leader like me? Or a loser like Henry? Do you want someone who will make you proud of this school? Or someone like Henry who will make you ashamed? *I* will be the best President ever. I'm already Captain of the Football Team. I know how to tell people what to do. This school will be heaven with me in charge. Remember, a vote for me will brighten every school day.'

'Go Margaret!' yelled Sour Susan as Margaret sat down.

Horrid Henry rose to speak.

'When I'm President,' said Horrid Henry, 'I promise a Goo-Shooter day! I promise a Gross-Out day! With my best friend Marvin the Maniac presenting the prize. School will start at lunchtime, and end after playtime. Gobble and Go will run the school cafeteria. I promise no homework! I promise skateboarding in the hall! I promise ice cream! And sweets!

'If you vote for Margaret, you'll get a dictator. And how do I know this? Because I have discovered her top-secret plans!' Horrid Henry pulled out a piece of paper covered in writing and showed it to the hall. 'Just listen to what she wrote:

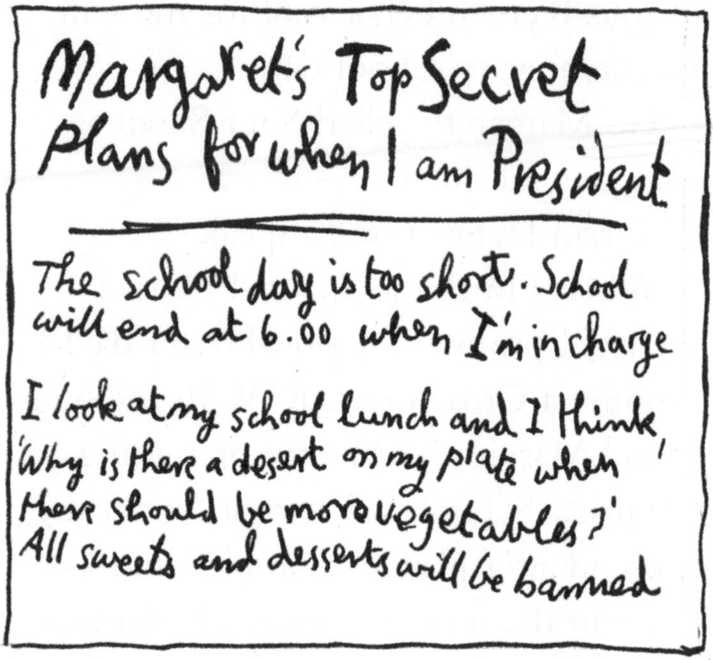
Margaret's Top Secret Plans for when I am President

The school day is too short. School will end at 6.00 when I'm in charge

I look at my school lunch and I think, 'Why is there a desert on my plate when there should be more vegetables?' All sweets and desserts will be banned

'I never wrote that!' screeched Margaret.

'She would say that, wouldn't she?' said Henry smoothly. 'But the voters need to know the truth.'

'He's lying!' shouted Margaret.

'Don't be fooled, everyone! Margaret will ban sweets! Margaret will ban crisps! Margaret will make you do lots more homework. Margaret wants to have school seven days a week.

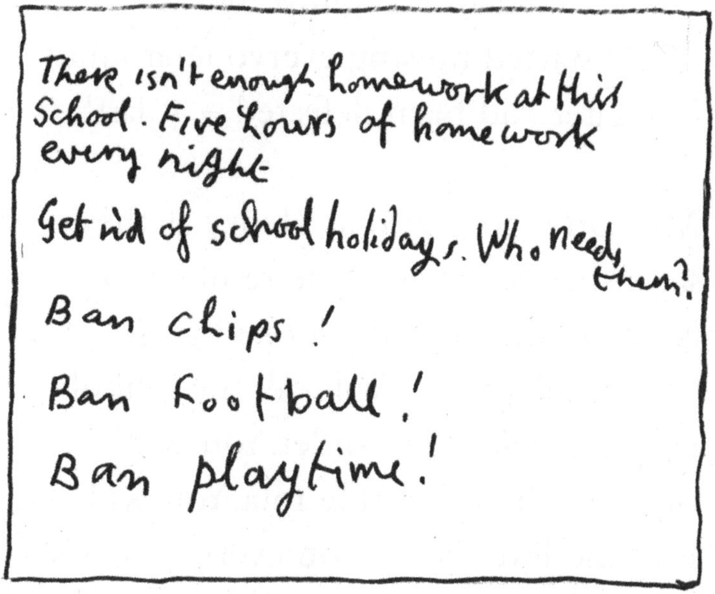
There isn't enough homework at this School. Five hours of homework every night
Get rid of school holidays. Who needs them?
Ban chips!
Ban football!
Ban playtime!

'So vote Henry if you want to stop this evil fiend! Vote Henry for loads of sweets! Vote Henry for loads of fun! Vote Henry for President!'

'Henry! Henry! Henry!' shouted Ralph, as Henry sat down to rapturous applause.

He'd done it! He'd won! And by a landslide. Yes!! He was President Lord High Master of the Universe! Just wait till he started bossing everyone around! Margaret had been defeated – at last!

Mrs Oddbod glared at Henry as they sat in her office after the results had been announced. She looked grey. 'As President, you will call the school council meeting to order. You will organise the toilet tidy rota. You will lead the litter collection every playtime.'

Horrid Henry's knees felt weak.

Toilet . . . tidy . . . rota? Litter? What?? *That* was his job? That's why he'd schemed and bribed and fought and campaigned and given away all those sweets?

Where was his throne? His title? His power?

NOOO!

'I resign!' said Horrid Henry.

3

HORRID HENRY'S BAD PRESENT

Ding dong.

'I'll get it!' shrieked Horrid Henry. He jumped off the sofa, pushed past Peter, ran to the door, and flung it open.

'Hi, Grandma,' said Horrid Henry. He looked at her hopefully. Yes! She was holding a huge carrier bag. Something lumpy and bumpy bulged inside. But not just any old something, like knitting or a spare jumper. Something big. Something ginormous. That meant . . . that meant . . . yippee!

Horrid Henry loved it when Grandma visited, because she often brought him a present. Mum and Dad gave really boring presents, like socks and dictionaries and games like Virtual Classroom and Name that Vegetable.

Grandma gave really great presents, like fire engines with wailing sirens, shrieking zombies with flashing lights, and once, even the Snappy Zappy Critters that Mum and Dad had said he couldn't have even if he begged for a million years.

'Where's my present?' said Horrid Henry, lunging for Grandma's bag. 'Gimme my present!'

'Don't be horrid, Henry,' said Mum, grabbing him and holding him back.

'I'm not being horrid, I just want my present,' said Henry, scowling. Why should he wait a second longer when it was obvious Grandma had some fantastic gift for him?

'Hi, Grandma,' said Peter. 'You know you don't need to bring *me* a present when you come to visit. You're the present.'

Horrid Henry's foot longed to kick Peter into the next room.

'Wait till *after* you get your present,' hissed his head.

'Good thinking,' said his foot.

'Thank you, Peter,' said Grandma. 'Now, have you been good boys?'

'I've been perfect,' said Peter. 'But Henry's been horrid.'

'Have not,' said Henry.

'Have too,' said Peter. 'Henry took all my crayons and melted them on the radiator.'

'That was an accident,' said Henry. 'How was I supposed to know they would melt? And next time get out of the hammock when you're told.'

'But it was my turn,' said Peter.

'Wasn't, you wormy worm toad–'

'Was too.'

'Right,' said Grandma. She reached into the bag and pulled out two gigantic dinosaurs. One Tyrannosaurus Rex was purple, the other was green.

'RAAAAAAAA,' roared one dinosaur, rearing and bucking and stretching out his blood-red claws.

'FEED ME!' bellowed the other,

shaking his head and gnashing his teeth.

Horrid Henry's heart stopped. His jaw dropped. His mouth opened to speak, but no sound came out.

Two Tyrannosaur Dinosaur Roars! Only the greatest toy ever in the history of the universe! Everyone wanted one. How had Grandma found them? They'd been sold out for weeks. Moody Margaret would die of jealousy when she saw Henry's T-Rex and heard it roaring and bellowing and stomping around the garden.

'Wow,' said Horrid Henry.

'Wow,' said Perfect Peter.

Grandma smiled. 'Who wants the purple one, and who wants the green one?'

That was a thought. Which one should he choose? Which T-Rex was the best?

Horrid Henry looked at the purple dinosaur.

Hmmm, thought Henry, I do love the colour purple.

Perfect Peter looked at the purple dinosaur.

Hmmm, thought Peter, those claws are a bit scary.

Horrid Henry looked at the green dinosaur.

Oooh, thought Henry. I like those red eyes.

Perfect Peter looked at the green dinosaur.

Oooh, thought Peter, those eyes are awfully red.

Horrid Henry sneaked a peek at Peter to see which dinosaur *he* wanted.

Perfect Peter sneaked a peek at Henry to see which dinosaur *he* wanted.

Then they pounced.

'I want the purple one,' said Henry, snatching it out of Grandma's hand. 'Purple rules.'

'*I* want the purple one,' said Peter.

'I said it first,' said Henry. He clutched the Tyrannosaurus tightly. How could he have hesitated for a moment? What was he thinking? The purple one was best. The green one was horrible. Who ever heard of a green T-Rex anyway?

Perfect Peter didn't know what to say. Henry *had* said it first. But the purple Tyrannosaurus was so obviously better than the green. Its teeth were pointier. Its scales were scalier. Its big clumpy feet were so much clumpier.

'I *thought* it first,' whimpered Peter.

Henry snorted. 'I thought it first, *and* I said it first. The purple one's mine,' he said. Just wait until he showed it to the

Purple Hand Gang. What a guard it would make.

Perfect Peter looked at the purple dinosaur.

Perfect Peter looked at the green dinosaur.

Couldn't he be perfect and accept the green one? The one Henry didn't want?

'But I'm obviously the best,' hissed the purple T-Rex. 'Who'd want the boring old green one? Bleccchhhh.'

'It's true, I'm not as good as the purple one,' sobbed the green dinosaur. 'The purple is for big boys, the green is for babies.'

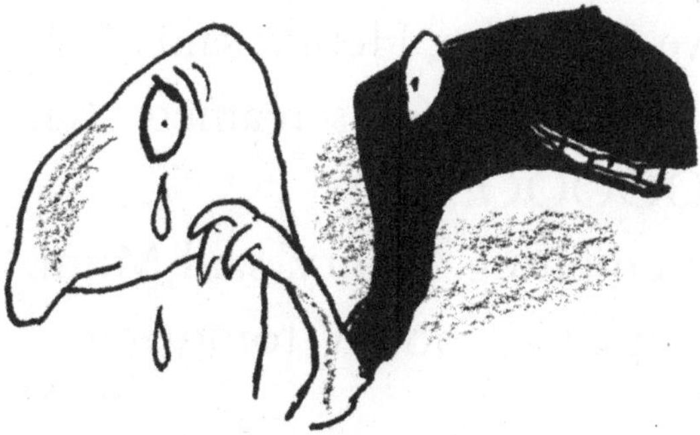

'I want the purple one!' wailed Peter. He started to cry.

'But they're exactly the same,' said Mum. 'They're just different colours.'

'I want the purple one!' screamed Henry and Peter.

'Oh dear,' said Grandma.

'Henry, you're the eldest, let Peter have the purple one,' said Dad.

WHAT?

'NO!' said Horrid Henry. 'It's mine.' He clutched it tightly.

'He's only little,' said Mum.

'So?' said Horrid Henry. 'It's not fair. I want the purple one!'

'Give it to him, Henry,' said Dad.

'NOOOOOOO!' screamed Henry. 'NOOOOOO!'

'I'm counting, Henry,' said Mum. 'No TV tonight . . . no TV tomorrow . . . no TV . . .'

'NOOOO!' screamed Horrid Henry. Then he hurled the purple dinosaur at Peter.

Henry could hardly believe what had just happened. Just because he was the oldest, he had to take the bad present? It was totally and utterly and completely unfair.

'I want the purple one!'

'You know that "I want doesn't get",' said Peter. 'Isn't that right, Mum?'

'It certainly is,' said Mum.

Horrid Henry pounced. He was a ginormous crocodile chomping on a very chewy child.

'AAAIIIEEEEE!' screamed Peter. 'Henry bit me.'

'Don't be horrid, Henry!' shouted Mum. 'Poor Peter.'

'Serves him right!' shrieked Horrid Henry. 'You're the meanest parents in the world and I hate you.'

'Go to your room!' shouted Dad.

'No pocket money for a week!' shouted Mum.

'Fine!' screamed Horrid Henry.

Horrid Henry sat in his bedroom. He glared at the snot-green dinosaur scowling at him from where he'd thrown it on the floor and stomped on it. He hated the colour green. He loved

the colour purple. The leader of the Purple Hand Gang deserved the purple Dinosaur Roar.

He'd make Peter swap dinosaurs if it was the last thing he did. And if Peter wouldn't swap, he'd be sorry he was born. Henry would ... Henry could ...

And then suddenly Horrid Henry had a wonderful, wicked idea. Why had he never thought of this before?

Perfect Peter sat in his bedroom. He smiled at the purple dinosaur as it lurched roaring around the room.

'RRRRAAAAAAAAAA! RAAAAAAAAAA! FEED ME!' bellowed the dinosaur.

How lucky he was to have the purple dinosaur. Purple was much better than green. It was only fair that Peter got the purple dinosaur, and Henry got the yucky green one. After all, Peter was perfect and Henry was horrid. Peter deserved the purple one.

Suddenly Horrid Henry burst into his bedroom.

'Mum said to stay in your room,' squealed Peter, shoving the dinosaur under his desk and standing guard in front of it. Henry would have to drag him away kicking and screaming before he got his hands on Peter's T-Rex.

'So?' said Henry.

'I'm telling on you,' said Peter.

'Go ahead,' said Henry. 'I'm telling on *you*, wibble pants.'

Tell on him? Tell what?

'There's nothing to tell,' said Perfect Peter.

'Oh yes there is,' said Henry. 'I'm going to tell everyone what a mean horrid wormy toad you are, stealing the purple dinosaur when I said I wanted it first.'

Perfect Peter gasped. Horrid? Him?

'I didn't steal it,' said Peter. 'And I'm not horrid.'

'Are too.'

'Am not. I'm perfect.'

'No you're not. If you were *really* perfect, you wouldn't be so selfish,' said Henry.

'I'm not selfish,' whimpered Peter.

But *was* he being selfish keeping the purple dinosaur, when Henry wanted it so badly?

'Mum and Dad said I could have it,' said Peter weakly.

'That's 'cause they knew you'd just start crying,' said Henry. 'Actually, they're disappointed in you. I heard them.'

'What did they say?' gasped Peter.

'That you were a crybaby,' said Henry.

'I'm not a crybaby,' said Peter.

'Then why are you acting like one, crybaby?'

Could Henry be telling the truth? Mum and Dad . . . disappointed in him . . . thinking he was a baby? A selfish baby? A *horrid* selfish baby?

Oh no, thought Peter. Could Henry be right? *Was* he being horrid?

'Go on, Peter,' urged his angel. 'Give Henry the purple one. After all, they're exactly the same, just different colours.'

'Don't do it!' urged his devil. 'Why should you always be perfect? Be horrid for once.'

'Uhmm, uhmm,' said Peter.

'You know you want to do the right thing,' said Henry.

Peter did want to do the right thing.

'Okay, Henry,' said Peter. 'You can have the purple dinosaur. I'll have the green one.'

YES!!!

Slowly Perfect Peter crawled under his desk and picked up the purple dinosaur.

'Good boy, Peter,' said his angel.

'Idiot,' said his devil.

Slowly Peter held out the dinosaur to Henry. Henry grabbed it . . .

Wait. Was he crazy? Why should he swap with Henry? Henry was only trying to trick him . . .

'Give it back!' yelled Peter.

'No!' said Henry.

Peter tugged on the dinosaur's legs.

Henry tugged on the dinosaur's head.

'Gimme!'

'Gimme!'

Tug

Tug

Yank

Yank

Snaaaaap.

Riiiiiiip.

Horrid Henry looked at the twisted purple dinosaur head in his hands.

Perfect Peter looked at the broken purple dinosaur claw in his hands.

'I want the green dinosaur!' shrieked Henry and Peter.

BURP!

4

HORRID HENRY WAKES THE DEAD

'No, no, no, no, no!' shouted Miss Battle-Axe. 'Spitting is not a talent, Graham. Violet, you can't do the Can-Can as your talent. Ralph, burping to the beat is not a talent.'

She turned to Bert. 'What's your talent?'

'I dunno,' said Beefy Bert.

'And what about you, Steven?' said Miss Battle-Axe grimly.

'Caveman,' grunted Stone-Age Steven. 'Ugg!'

Horrid Henry had had enough.

'Me next!' shrieked Horrid Henry. 'I've got a great talent! Me next!'

'Me!' shrieked Moody Margaret.

'Me!' shrieked Rude Ralph.

'No one who shouts out will be performing *anything*,' said Miss Battle-Axe.

Next week was Horrid Henry's school talent show. But this wasn't an ordinary school talent show. Oh no. This year was different. This year, the famous TV presenter Sneering Simone was choosing the winner.

But best and most fantastic of all, the prize was a chance to appear on Simone's TV programme *Talent Tigers*. And from there . . . well, there was no end to the fame and fortune which awaited the winner.

Horrid Henry had to win. He just had to. A chance to be on TV! A chance for his genius to be recognised, at last.

The only problem was, he had so many talents it was impossible to pick just one. He could eat crisps faster than Greedy Graham. He could burp to the theme tune of *Marvin the Maniac*. He could stick out his tongue almost as far as Moody Margaret.

But brilliant as these talents were, perhaps they weren't *quite* special enough to win. Hmmmm . . .

Wait, he had it.

He could perform his new rap, 'I have

an ugly brother, ick ick ick/ A smelly toad brother, who makes me sick.' That would be sure to get him on *Talent Tigers*.

'Margaret!' barked Miss Battle-Axe, 'what's your talent?'

'Susan and I are doing a rap,' said Moody Margaret.

What?

'*I'm* doing a rap,' howled Henry. How dare Margaret steal his idea!

'Only one person can do a rap,' said Miss Battle-Axe firmly.

'Unfair!' shrieked Horrid Henry.

'Be quiet, Henry,' said Miss Battle-Axe.

Moody Margaret stuck out her tongue at Horrid Henry. 'Nah nah ne nah nah.'

Horrid Henry stuck out his tongue at Moody Margaret. Aaaarrgh! It was so unfair.

'I'm doing a hundred push-ups,' said Aerobic Al.

'I'm playing the drums,' said Jazzy Jim.

'I want to do a rap!' howled Horrid Henry. 'Mine's much better than hers!'

'You have to do something else or not take part,' said Miss Battle-Axe, consulting her list.

Not take part? Was Miss Battle-Axe out of her mind? Had all those years working on a chain gang done her in?

Miss Battle-Axe stood in front of Henry, baring her fangs. Her pen tapped impatiently on her notebook.

'Last chance, Henry. List closes in ten seconds . . .'

What to do, what to do?

'I'll do magic,' said Horrid Henry.

How hard could it be to do some magic? He wasn't a master of disguise and the fearless leader of the Purple Hand Gang for nothing. In fact, not only would he do magic, he would do the greatest magic trick the world had ever seen. No rabbits out of a hat. No flowers out of a cane. No sawing a girl in half – though if Margaret volunteered Henry would be very happy to oblige.

No! He, Henry, Il Stupendioso, the greatest magician ever, would . . . would . . . he would wake the dead.

Wow. That was much cooler than a rap. He could see it now. He would chant his magic spells and wave his magic wand, until slowly, slowly, slowly, out of the coffin the bony body would rise, sending the audience screaming out of the hall!

Yes! thought Horrid Henry, *Talent Tigers* here I come. All he needed was an assistant.

Unfortunately, no one in his class wanted to assist him.

'Are you crazy?' said Gorgeous Gurinder.

'I've got a much better talent than *that*. No way,' said Clever Clare.

'Wake the dead?' gasped Weepy William. 'Nooooo.'

Rats, thought Horrid Henry. For his spectacular trick to work, an assistant was essential. Henry hated working with other children, but sometimes it couldn't be helped. Was there anyone he knew who would do exactly as they were told? Someone who would obey his every order? Hmmm. Perhaps there was a certain someone who would even pay for the privilege of being in his show.

Perfect Peter was busy emptying the dishwasher without being asked.

'Peter,' said Henry sweetly, 'how much would you pay me if I let you be in my magic show?'

Perfect Peter couldn't believe his ears. Henry was asking him to be in his show. Peter had always wanted to be in a show. And now Henry was actually asking him after he'd said no a million times. It was a dream come true. He'd pay anything.

'I've got £6.27 in my piggy bank,' said Peter eagerly.

Horrid Henry pretended to think.

'Done!' said Horrid Henry. 'You can start by painting the coffin black.'

'Thank you, Henry,' said Peter humbly, handing over the money.

Tee hee, thought Horrid Henry, pocketing the loot.

Henry told Peter what he had to do. Peter's jaw dropped.

'And will my name be on the billboard so everyone will know I'm your assistant?' asked Peter.

'Of course,' said Horrid Henry.

*

The great day arrived at last. Henry had practised and practised and practised. His magic robes were ready. His magic spells were ready. His coffin was ready. His props were ready. Even his dead body was as ready as it would ever be. Victory was his!

Henry and Peter stood backstage and peeked through the curtain as the audience charged into the hall. The school was buzzing. Parents pushed and shoved to get the best seats. There was a stir as Sneering Simone swept in, taking her seat in the front row.

'Would you *please* move?' demanded

Margaret's mother, waving her camcorder. 'I can't see my little Maggie Muffin.'

'And I can't see Al with *your* big head in the way,' snapped Aerobic Al's dad, shoving his camera in front of Moody Margaret's mum.

'Parents, behave!' shouted Mrs Oddbod. 'What an exciting programme we have for you today! You will be amazed at all the talents in this school. First Clare will recite Pi, which as you all know is the ratio of the circumference of a circle to the diameter, to 31 significant figures!'

'3.14159 26535 89793 23846 26433 83279,' said Clever Clare.

Sneering Simone made a few notes.

'Boring,' shouted Horrid Henry. 'Boring!'

'Shhh,' hissed Miss Battle-Axe.

'Now, Gurinder, Linda, Fiona and Zoe proudly present: the cushion dance!'

Gorgeous Gurinder, Lazy Linda, Fiery Fiona and Zippy Zoe ran on stage and placed a cushion in each corner. Then they skipped to each pillow, pretended to sew it, then hopped around with a pillow each, singing:

'We're the stitching queens
dressed in sateen,
we're full of beans,
see us preen,
as we steal . . . the . . . scene!'

Sneering Simone looked surprised. Tee hee, thought Horrid Henry gleefully. If everyone's talents were as awful as that, he was a shoe-in for *Talent Tigers*.

'Lovely,' said Mrs Oddbod. 'Just lovely. And now we have William, who will play the flute.'

Weepy William put his mouth to the flute and blew. There was no sound.

William stopped and stared at his flute. The mouth hole appeared to have vanished.

Everyone was looking at him. What could he do?

'Toot toot toot,' trilled William, pretending to blow. 'Toot toot toot-waaaaaah!' wailed William, bursting into tears and running off stage.

'Never mind,' said Mrs Oddbod, 'anyone could put the mouthpiece on upside down. And now we have . . .' Mrs Oddbod glanced at her paper, 'a caveman Ugga Ugg dance.'

Stone-Age Steven and Beefy Bert stomped on stage wearing leopard-skin costumes and carrying clubs.

'UGGG!' grunted Stone-Age Steven. 'UGGG UGGG UGGG UGGG UGGG! Me cave man!'

STOMP CLUMPA CLUMP
STOMP CLUMPA CLUMP

stomped Stone-Age Steven.

STOMP CLUMPA CLUMP
STOMP CLUMPA CLUMP

stomped Beefy Bert.

'UGGA BUG UGGA BUG UGG UGG UGG,' bellowed Steven, whacking the floor with his club.

'Bert!' hissed Miss Battle-Axe. 'This isn't your talent! What are you doing on stage?'

'I dunno,' said Beefy Bert.

'Boo! Boooooo!' jeered Horrid Henry from backstage as the Cavemen thudded off.

Then Moody Margaret and Sour Susan performed their rap:

'Mar-garet, ooh ooh oooh
Mar-garet, it's all true
Mar-garet, best of the best
Pick Margaret, and dump the rest.'

Rats, thought Horrid Henry, glaring. My rap was so much better. What a waste. And why was the audience applauding?

'Booooo!' yelled Horrid Henry. 'Boooooo!'

'Another sound out of you and you will not be performing,' snapped Miss Battle-Axe.

'And now Soraya will be singing "You broke my heart in 39 pieces", accompanied by her mother on the piano,' said Mrs Oddbod hastily.

'Sing out, Soraya!' hissed her mother, pounding the piano and singing along.

'I'm singing as loud as I can,' yelled Soraya.

BANG! BANG! BANG! BANG! BANG! BANG! went the piano.

Then Jolly Josh began to saw 'Twinkle twinkle little star' on his double bass.

Sneering Simone held her ears.

'We're next,' said Horrid Henry, grabbing hold of his billboard and whipping off the cloth.

Perfect Peter stared at the billboard. It read:

Il Stupendioso, world's greatest magician played by Henry

Magic by Henry
Costumes by Henry
Props by Henry
Sound by Henry
Written by Henry
Directed by Henry

'But Henry,' said Peter, 'where's my name?'

'Right here,' said Horrid Henry, pointing.

On the back, in tiny letters, was written:

Assistant: Peter

'But no one will see that,' said Peter.

Henry snorted.

'If I put your name on the *front* of the billboard, everyone would guess the trick,' said Henry.

'No they wouldn't,' said Peter.

Honestly, thought Horrid Henry, did

any magician ever have such a dreadful helper?

'I'm the star,' said Henry. 'You're lucky you're even in my show. Now shut up and get in the coffin.'

Perfect Peter was furious. That was just like Henry, to be so mean.

'Get in!' ordered Henry.

Peter put on his skeleton mask and climbed into the coffin. He was fuming.

Henry had said he'd put his name on the billboard, and then he'd written it on the back. No one would know he was the assistant. No one.

The lights dimmed. Spooky music began to play.

'Ooooooooohhhh,' moaned the ghostly sounds as Horrid Henry, wearing his special long black robes studded with stars and a special magician's hat, dragged his coffin through the curtains onto the stage.

'I am Il Stupendioso, the great and powerful magician!' intoned Henry. 'Now, Il Stupendioso will perform the greatest trick ever seen. Be prepared to marvel. Be prepared to be amazed. Be prepared not to believe your eyes. I, Il Stupendioso, will wake the dead!!'

'Ooohh,' gasped the audience.

Horrid Henry swept back and forth across the stage, waving his wand and mumbling.

'First I will say the secret words of magic. Beware! Beware! Do not try this at home. Do not try this in a graveyard. Do not – ' Henry's voice sank to a whisper – 'do not try this unless you're prepared for the dead . . . to walk!' Horrid Henry ended his sentence with a blood-curdling scream. The audience gasped.

Horrid Henry stood above the coffin and chanted:

'Abracadabra,
flummery flax,

voodoo hoodoo
mumbo crax.
Rise and shine, corpse of mine!'

Then Horrid Henry whacked the coffin once with his wand.

Slowly Perfect Peter poked a skeleton hand out of the coffin, then withdrew it.

'Ohhhh,' went the audience. Toddler Tom began to wail.

Horrid Henry repeated the spell.

'Abracadabra,
flummery flax,
voodoo hoodoo
mumbo crax.
Rise and shine, bony swine!'

Then Horrid Henry whacked the coffin twice with his wand.

This time Perfect Peter slowly raised the plastic skull with a few tufts of blond hair glued to it, then lowered it back down. Toddler Tom began to howl.

'And now, for the third and final time, I will say the magic spell, and before your eyes, the body will rise. Stand back . . .'

'Abracadabra,
flummery flax,
voodoo hoodoo
mumbo crax.
Rise and shine, here is the sign!'

And Horrid Henry whacked the coffin three times with his wand.

The audience held its breath.

And held it.

And held it.

And held it.

'He's been dead a long time, maybe his hearing isn't so good,' said Horrid Henry. 'Rise and shine, here is the sign,' shouted Henry, whacking the coffin furiously.

Again, nothing happened.

'Rise and shine, brother of mine,' hissed Henry, kicking the coffin, 'or you'll be sorry you were born.'

I'm on strike, thought Perfect Peter. How dare Henry stick his name on the back of the billboard. And after all Peter's hard work!

Horrid Henry looked at the audience. The audience looked expectantly at Horrid Henry.

What could he do? Open the coffin and yank the body out? Yell, 'Ta da!' and run off stage? Do his famous elephant dance?

Horrid Henry took a deep breath.

'Now that's what I call *dead*,' said Horrid Henry.

'This was a difficult decision,' said Sneering Simone. Henry held his breath. He'd kill Peter later. Peter had finally risen from the coffin *after* Henry left the stage, then instead of slinking off, he'd actually said, 'Hello everyone! I'm alive!' and waved. Grrr. Well, Peter wouldn't have to pretend to be a corpse once Henry had finished with him.

'. . . a very difficult decision. But I've decided that the winner is . . .' Please not Margaret, please not Margaret, prayed Henry. Sneering Simone consulted her notes, 'The winner is the Il Stupendioso–'

'YES!!' screamed Horrid Henry, leaping to his feet. He'd done it! Fame at last! Henry Superstar was born! Yes yes yes!

Sneering Simone glared. 'As I was saying, the Il Stupendioso corpse. Great comic timing. Can someone tell me his name?'

Horrid Henry stopped dancing.

Huh?

What?

The *corpse*?

'Is that me?' said Peter. '*I* won?'

'NOOOOOOOOOO!' shrieked Horrid Henry.

HORRID HENRY BOOKS

Horrid Henry
Horrid Henry and the Secret Club
Horrid Henry Tricks the Tooth Fairy
Horrid Henry's Nits
Horrid Henry Gets Rich Quick
Horrid Henry's Haunted House
Horrid Henry and the Mummy's Curse
Horrid Henry's Revenge
Horrid Henry and the Bogey Babysitter
Horrid Henry's Stinkbomb
Horrid Henry's Underpants
Horrid Henry Meets the Queen
Horrid Henry and the Mega-Mean Time Machine
Horrid Henry and the Football Fiend
Horrid Henry and the Abominable Snowman
Horrid Henry Robs the Bank
Horrid Henry Wakes the Dead
Horrid Henry Rocks
Horrid Henry and the Zombie Vampire
Horrid Henry's Monster Movie
Horrid Henry's Nightmare
Horrid Henry's Krazy Ketchup

Colour books

Horrid Henry's Big Bad Book
Horrid Henry's Wicked Ways
Horrid Henry's Evil Enemies
Horrid Henry Rules the World
Horrid Henry's House of Horrors
Horrid Henry's Dreadful Deeds
Horrid Henry Shows Who's Boss

Joke Books

Horrid Henry's Joke Book
Horrid Henry's Jolly Joke Book
Horrid Henry's Mighty Joke Book
Horrid Henry Versus Moody Margaret
Horrid Henry's Hilariously Horrid Joke Book
Horrid Henry's Purple Hand Gang Joke Book

Early Readers

Don't Be Horrid, Henry!
Horrid Henry's Birthday Party
Horrid Henry's Holiday
Horrid Henry's Underpants
Horrid Henry Gets Rich Quick
Horrid Henry and the Football Fiend
Horrid Henry's Nits
Horrid Henry and Moody Margaret
Horrid Henry's Thank You Letter
Horrid Henry Reads a Book
Horrid Henry's Car Journey

Horrid Henry is also available on CD and as a digital download, all read by Miranda Richardson.